The
No Delay
Cafe

D1571936

Cover photo and design by Chinle Miller.

ISBN: 978-0-9849356-4-2
Yellow Cat and the accompanying logo are registered trademarks owned by Yellow Cat Publishing.

www.yellowcatbooks.com

· F O R ·

Bud and Melyssa Shumway

CHAPTER 1

Bud Shumway was standing in an irrigation ditch, waiting for the water to arrive, having just opened the headgate on up the ditch a ways.

He reached into the front pocket of his khaki shirt and pulled out the little metal clicker device his wife, Wilma Jean, had received in the mail that morning. He read the package label before opening it:

"Clicker training is an operant conditioning method for training a dog by using a small mechanical noisemaker as a marker for behavior. The clicker tells the dog that a certain behavior is wanted. Press the clicker when your dog does what you want him to."

Now Bud tried to open the package, cussing whoever had deemed it necessary to make sure everything was overly wrapped—probably some scissors manufacturer—then managed to pull the plastic wrapping off just as the head of irrigation water reached his feet, a brownish foam breaking against the toes of his waterproof Herman Survivor boots.

He'd left his irrigating boots home by accident, as he'd been too busy thinking about Wilma Jean's threat to make him start eating more salads if his Levis got any tighter. He knew he was going to have to cut back on the doughnuts at the Chow Down for his morning break.

The reason Bud was standing in the ditch was that he was waiting to make sure the irrigation gate he'd opened a bit earlier wasn't clogged and water would come on down to the melon field. Now that the planting was done, irrigating was about the only chore he would have here for a couple of months, other than making sure the two seasonal guys he'd hired kept the weeds down.

He finally got the clicker free of the plastic, then immediately began pressing the small metal device over and over. It made a somewhat abrasive yet satisfying clicking noise, just as advertised.

The clicker was Wilma Jean's latest ploy in trying to get their Bassett hound, Hoppie, and their dachshund, Pierre, to comply with certain simple directives—things like staying down off the kitchen table when nobody was looking (which admittedly was more Hoppie's doing than Pierre's, as Pierre was too short to climb up there) and not chewing on Wilma Jean's sheepskin slippers (she was now on her third pair, and the main suspect here was Pierre).

Bud figured the clicker would be just another in a useless string of training attempts, and he suspected this because he knew neither he nor Wilma Jean had the disciplinarian mindset one needed to properly train bad little dogs.

In fact, he himself thought it was kind of exceptional that Hoppie had managed to get up on the table, and Bud was secretly proud of Hoppie's deductional skills or whatever one called it when a dog figured out where the really good food was located and then managed to get himself to it.

Bud figured this skill would come in handy if he and Hoppie ever got lost out in that big desert just out of town, as Hoppie would immediately take them both to the nearest food source.

Bud stood there awhile, practicing clicking, first doing it slow, then fast, while the irrigation foam washed over his boots and was finally followed by real water.

By the time he noticed what was happening, his pant cuffs were wet and the water was running pretty fast, threatening to top over the bottom laces of his boots, where the waterproofing did little good.

As Bud scrambled out of the ditch, his cell phone rang. He could tell from the caller ID that it was his ex-deputy, Howie, who had become sheriff when Bud resigned due to burnout, taking up melon farming.

Bud had continued on in the capacity of Howie's unpaid consultant, as Howie managed to call him at least once a day with questions. But Bud didn't mind, as Howie had been a deputy for only a few months before becoming sheriff, and he didn't have much experience.

Before that, Howie had run his little drive-in, called *Howie's*, which was just across the street from the sheriff's office there in the little town of Green River, Utah.

"Yell-ow," Bud answered as he stood on the edge of the ditch, watching the water now coursing on down to the newly planted melon fields.

"Sheriff, I need to talk to you," Howie said.

"What's going on, Howie?"

Bud expected to have to wait a bit for Howie to reply, as Howie seemed to enjoy making him guess, some kind of power play maybe, or perhaps Howie was just thinking, but this time, Howie was right on it.

"I got this letter in the mail today, Sheriff, and it's kinda weird."

"How so, Sheriff?" Bud replied, trying to remind Howie that he, Howie, was now the sheriff.

Bud patiently waited, knowing Howie would tell him only when he was ready—kind of like when Bud pestered Wilma Jean about what was for dinner, but again, Howie didn't hesitate.

"Well, all it has is a piece of paper with some numbers on it, which I think might be coordinates. And then there's this, well, this weird thing. I'm wondering if maybe it isn't some kind of threat or something, Sheriff. I'd sure like you to take a look at it."

"A threat? What kind of weird thing, Howie?" Bud sighed.

Howie was never going to quit calling him sheriff, he figured. He might just as well give up and accept it.

"Well, it looks like a claw, like something from a weird horror movie. Problem is, it's hard as a rock. And someone wrote on the envelope, 'Hand stamp.' What does that mean?" Howie seemed a bit disturbed.

"It means they didn't want it going through the automatic postage machine, Howie. It has something they didn't want broken. But why would it be a threat?"

"Well, you know, you get a weird claw in the mail with mysterious coordinates, and what if it's from some devil's worshippers or someone like that? Or worse yet, something to do with aliens? Someone trying to lure you out there to the middle of nowhere."

"Aliens?"

"Yeah, there's been talk about flying saucers around here. Old Man Green said he saw one trying to round up his cattle, you know, that same old rancher I helped when some of his steers went missing awhile ago."

"I remember that—the ones that weren't really missing, but had mud on their faces so they looked different. He's probably on the sauce again, Howie."

Bud paused. He really didn't want to get involved in law enforcement business, as he had irrigation needing done, but he knew Howie needed reassurance, being fairly new and all.

Howie continued, "And Sheriff, someone's been calling all morning, but when I answer, they just hang up."

Bud had to admit this sounded a bit strange. He replied, "You can always get in touch with the phone company to trace who called." He paused, then added, "Well, come on out to the farm here and bring the letter with you. We'll take a look."

"Thanks, Sheriff. I don't know how I'd do this job without you. You sure you don't wanna come back? You could hire on as my deputy."

"No, that's OK, Howie, but I appreciate it. I really do."

"OK, Sheriff, but that's a standing offer, you know that." 10-4, over and out."

CHAPTER 2

It wasn't long before Howie drove up to the Krider Melon Farm in an old black and white police cruiser that had the words "Emery County Sheriff" on the side. Bud was surprised, as the old Ford Crown Victoria had pretty much been mothballed when the sheriff's office had bought a new Toyota Land Cruiser.

As usual, Howie's long lanky legs took a bit longer to get out of the car than the rest of him, and Bud thought Howie looked like he'd put on a bit of weight since he'd last seen him, which Howie could use, unlike Bud. Must be all that good home cookin' since he and his ex-wife, Maureen, got remarried, Bud figured.

"Howdy, Sheriff," Howie said, grinning at Bud. "Looks like you've been playing in the water." Howie nodded at Bud's wet pant legs, then handed him an envelope.

Bud studied it for a minute, then noted, "It's postmarked Radium. Why would someone down there be interested in the Sheriff of Emery County, Howie? You really think it's some kind of threat?"

Howie now looked serious. "Open it, Sheriff, then you'll see what I'm talking about."

Bud opened the letter, and sure enough, it contained a small thin piece of paper with what looked like coordinates written on it: *39°11'14"N   110°34'32"W*

Bud examined the paper. It had the words "GI Jay" printed on a military-type green and brown camouflage print. He knew it was a fairly common cigarette rolling paper, as he'd seen some of the guys down at the American Legion using it.

"Roll your own," Bud nodded to Howie.

Howie replied, "Yeah, and it's camouflaged, like maybe they were trying to hide something, like their identity. Someone's trying to be secretive and stealthy, Sheriff."

Bud now shook the envelope, and a four-inch claw slipped into his hand. He let out a low whistle.

"Look at that—it's a petrified dinosaur claw, Howie, and a big one, too."

"Petrified? You mean it's not real?"

"Well, sure it's real. It's just really old. And like you said, hard as a rock, because it is a rock."

"Why would someone send me a dinosaur claw and some coordinates?"

"Maybe they found something there and want you to go take a look," Bud answered.

"Like a dinosaur?"

"That would be my first guess," Bud replied.

"Well I'll be go to heck, Sheriff. Isn't it illegal to find dinosaur bones?"

"Well, the finding isn't so illegal, Howie, but the digging is. Maybe it's a tip that there's someone out there illegally digging bone. Or maybe someone found some bones and are worried about getting in trouble, so they're telling you where it is."

"Telling me? I would never dig dino bones, Sheriff. I'm the sheriff, and I sure wouldn't want to get myself in trouble." Howie grinned, then continued, "I'd have to arrest myself, and that could be a little awkward. 'Drop that bone, Sheriff. This is the sheriff, and you're under arrest.' I'd be so surprised I'd probably drop the bone on my foot, then I wouldn't be able to walk, making it impossible to arrest myself. And then where would Emery County be with a sheriff who couldn't walk?"

Bud laughed, though it was a bit strained. "It wouldn't much matter if you could walk or not if you were in jail, Howie. But look, if it is a bone site, they're probably thinking you might tell the museum up in Price or a paleontologist, someone licensed to dig. That would be my guess, that it's a bone site, and whoever found it doesn't want anyone to know they've been out bone hunting. I guess we could go take a look, but not in that old Crown Vic. Where's the Land Cruiser?"

"It's at the shop getting fixed. I kind of accidentally backed into a rock."

"Well, OK, we can take my rig. I need to stop at the house and get a few things, and we can check my atlas for those coordinates, see where we're going."

"So you don't think it's some weird cult thing?" Howie sounded a bit disappointed.

"Can't say for sure, Howie, but probably not."

"Well, OK," Howie replied, "But I can tell you I'm for sure gonna keep my guard up."

"Probably not a bad idea, in any case," Bud answered.

• • •

They were soon at Bud and Wilma Jean's house, a nice old bungalow on the edge of town with big trees surrounding a big grassy yard and old barn.

Bud ducked inside, where he quickly made a couple of ham sandwiches and filled a jug with water, then stuck his Ruger in its shoulder holster along with some ammo. He decided to leave Wilma Jean a note saying he'd gone out with Howie.

The dogs were gone, so Bud figured they were with Wilma Jean out running around town, such that there was to run around. There wasn't much to the little desert town of Green River, unless you liked creosote brush and coyotes, but the dogs liked cruising around in Wilma Jean's big pink Lincoln Continental, the one she'd won for selling Mary Kay cosmetics when they lived in Radium.

Bud wondered what was on tonight's dinner menu. He scribbled the words "the kids want meatballs tonight" on the corner of his note. Wilma Jean would be more likely to make it if she thought the dogs wanted it, Bud figured. Ever since Bud's new aunt-in-law LuAnn had fed him spaghetti and meatballs at the Paradox Cafe, he'd been craving them.

Bud now swung the screen door open, wondering if aunt-in-law was a valid kinship term, then wondered what his uncle Junior and LuAnn were up to over in the Paradox Valley. Maybe they'd come pay him and Wilma Jean a visit one of these days, Bud hoped.

He immediately turned and went back inside, grabbing his Utah atlas—he'd almost forgot to check out the coordinates in Howie's letter. He sat and studied the map for a bit, then got up and went back out the door. Bud knew this part of Utah like the back of his hand, so it hadn't taken him long to figure out where they were going and how to get there.

Howie was waiting in Bud's Toyota FJ, tapping his fingers on the dash and singing as Bud got in.

"Hey, Sheriff," Howie said, "We have a practice session tomorrow night over at the old fire station. You should come on over and listen to us. We need some feedback, though I think we're doing pretty good, myself. Barry thinks he may be able to get us a wedding gig over in Elmo soon."

"That would be great, Howie. I'd love to come over, but I promised Wilma Jean I'd help her at the bowling alley. She's got a new set of leagues starting up and needs me to register everyone."

Bud got a kick out of the fact that Howie and his wife had started a country-swing band.

"That's OK. Maybe next time," Howie replied. "Wanna hear the lyrics to my latest song?"

"Sure," Bud said as he backed the FJ out of the drive and turned towards town.

Howie continued, "You know that old Billy Walker song, 'I'm Down to my Last Cigarette'? You know, that old classic? Well, it inspired me to write one kinda like it, though the tune's different, but it's still honky tonk. Wanna hear it?"

Bud knew Howie was still a bit insecure about his musical abilities, in spite of his and Maureen's success so far with the Ramblin' Road Rangers, so he always tried to be encouraging.

"Sure, Howie, I really would like to hear it," he said again patiently.

"It's called, 'I'm Down to My Last Wad of Chew.' It's still kind of a rough draft, so don't be shy to tell me if you don't like it. It goes like this:"

Well, I'm down to my last wad of chew,
And honey, you know I'm sure blue.
You walked out on me,
And you took my car key,
And I'm down to my last wad of chew.
See, I'm down to my last wad of chew,
I thought that our love would be true,
My checkbook is gone,
Sweetheart you're a con,
And I'm down to my last wad of chew.

Bud grinned and said, "Howie, that one's gonna be a hit, I just know it." He was now driving west on the freeway.

"Thanks, Sheriff," Howie replied. "You know, we sure could use a drummer. It's just me on guitar and vocals, Maureen on honky tonk piano, and Barry on bass guitar. Why don't you join up with us and play drums? You could practice all day out on those melons. Maybe add a little bongo effect to the band."

"Well, now there's a thought, Howie," Bud replied. "A country-swing band with a bongo effect. I never considered myself a drummer, but you just never know where life's gonna lead, now do you?"

"Nope, you sure don't. But speaking of leading, you have any idea where we're going?"

"I do, Howie. I know pretty much where those coordinates are—it's out on the Green River Cutoff Road. I'd like to stop at the No Delay Cafe and grab a quick cup of coffee, since we'll be going right by there, if that's OK with you."

"Fine by me," Howie answered.

Bud exited the freeway after a few miles and headed north on Highway 191 towards Price. The highway and railroad tracks hung together, and he and Howie crossed a railroad bridge and saw a long freight train hauling coal from the mines over near Paonia, Colorado.

They drove on, following the flanks of the Bookcliffs, Mt. Elliot high above them, a giant point reminding everyone that the big Utah sky was just right up there.

It wasn't long until they came to what looked to be an old gas station remodeled into a cafe, where Bud made a quick turn off the highway, almost getting run over by a big semi in the process—a big semi with the words, "Utah State Patrol Safety Awareness Truck" on its side. It honked and drove on, the driver not even appearing to have touched his brakes.

CHAPTER 3

"Dang it, Sheriff, I saw that truck almost hit you. I've told the highway department a million times we need a turn lane out there. You can't see a darn thing, the way this place sits in a dip."

Bud and Howie sat in the old dilapidated back booth of the No Delay Cafe while the owner, Ray, took their order.

Bud replied, "I know, Ray. Isn't that how you and Wanda came to buy this place? Seems like the previous owner got tired of watching people about get run over, so he put it up for sale."

"Guess you'd better not delay when you turn into the No Delay Cafe," Howie offered.

Ray ignored Howie and answered Bud, "Yeah, that would be old Floyd Simpson, and he neglected to tell us about that aspect of things. One guy actually got hit, but he survived. Worst thing about it is that you can't see the cafe until you're right on it, so nobody stops, even though we put up signs down the road both ways. Last I heard, old Floyd was managing the Elks Club up in Price. So, what'll it be for you boys today? Nice to have some customers for a change."

Bud ordered coffee and a doughnut (he decided he'd start his diet tomorrow), while Howie ordered a hamburger and fries.

It wasn't long before their order arrived, and Ray leaned and whispered into Bud's ear as he sat a cup of coffee on the table. "Sheriff, can I talk to you for a minute in the back?"

Bud was surprised, but got up and followed Ray into the kitchen.

"Sorry to be so secretive, Sheriff, but I need to talk to you in private. Nothing against your deputy there, but I'd just as soon nobody else knew."

"That's fine, Ray. What's up?"

"Well, Bud, you know me and Wanda go way back—maybe too far back. She's been threatenin' to leave me for years, but I'm wonderin' if maybe today wasn't the day she made good on it. Things have been really tight lately, seems like nobody hardly ever stops. We had a little spat this mornin'—she's always sayin' I take her for granted, and I probably do. She took off on Buck, said she was goin' out for a little ride, and I ain't seen her since. I'm worried sick."

"Does she do this very often?" Bud asked.

"Yeah, she rides a lot, but usually just for an hour or two, then she's back. I guess it's kind of her way of de-stressin'. But she's been gone since about seven this mornin'. I tried callin' your office several times, but your deputy would always answer, and I wanted to talk to you, so I hung up."

"Ray, my deputy is now the sheriff. I resigned quite some time ago."

"You're kiddin' me! Resigned? Why would a good sheriff like you just go and resign?"

"I got burned out, Ray. It's a tough job, and I had an offer from Professor Krider to manage his melon farm there by the river."

"Well, I'll be go to. You're runnin' a farm now? So, I guess this means I'll have to deal with your deputy if Wanda don't show up?"

"He's doing a fine job, Ray. If Wanda turns up missing, he'll do as good a job as I would finding her." Bud paused, then added, "And he calls me about every day for advice, so I'm kind of still working the job, if you know what I mean. But Howie's going to eventually be a fine lawman. What does Wanda's horse look like?"

"It's a real pretty buckskin Quarter Horse, about 16 hands, kind of rangy. How she gets up on him is beyond me, as short as she is."

"Well, we're going out in the back country as soon as we leave here, so I'll keep an eye out. Any idea which way she rode?"

"She always cuts across the hills and meets up with the Green River Cutoff. Stays by the road. No traffic to speak of."

"We're going that way. I'll watch for her."

Bud turned and walked back into the cafe, sitting back down in the booth. Howie looked curious, and Bud noted he'd managed to wolf down his hamburger while waiting.

Bud explained, "Ray's wife, Wanda, took off riding this morning and hasn't come back. He's the one who was calling the office and hanging up."

"Why'd he hang up?" Howie asked through a mouthful of fries.

"He's kind of upset, you know, worried and all, nervous," Bud replied.

"Well, that's understandable."

Just then, Ray came out of the kitchen to refresh their coffee.

"You boys hear about the UFO that hovered over the cafe a couple of nights ago?" he asked.

"Whooeee," Howie replied, looking pointedly at Bud. "What happened?"

"Well, Sheriff," Ray said to Howie, "I almost called your office, but it wouldn't have done any good, cause it was gone before I could get to the phone. By the way, my wife's out riding and usually isn't gone this long, so keep an eye out for her. I tried calling your office a few times, but hung up. I apologize for that."

"It's OK," Howie said distractedly. "What did the UFO look like?"

"I don't actually know, cause by the time I got outside, it was gone. But there was this big eerie glow all around the cafe. It lit up everything outside. Scared the bejeebers outta me."

Howie looked again at Bud, then said, "See, Sheriff, I told you there were UFOs around. Maybe it has something to do with his wife missing."

Ray looked shocked. "You don't think so, do you?"

Bud replied, "Now, Ray, I betcha Wanda's just having too much fun to come home, maybe taking a new way back. All this talk about UFOs is just that, talk."

Bud fingered the clicker in his pocket. He had an uncontrollable urge to click it, but restrained himself.

"The one that hovered over the cafe wasn't just talk," Ray answered. "And there's been this strange guy comin' in every day. He eats, then just sits around, as if waiting."

"How so?" Bud asked.

"Well, he sits there and when someone comes in, you can tell he's listenin', almost like he's spyin' around. He told me he's camped somewhere on the Green River Cutoff. Says he's doing some research. Maybe he's an ALF. Well, I'll be danged. Speak of the devil and he shows up."

The cafe door opened, and a man wearing a sandstone-colored Carhart jacket walked in. He had dark longish hair and looked unkept, though fit, like someone used to being in the outback. He nodded hello to everyone, then sat in a booth and opened the menu.

Sure enough, he then held his menu aside and turned a bit, as if listening. Bud could see a white Ford pickup through the cafe window.

Bud said, "Well, we need to get going. Nice talking to you, Ray, and we'll sure keep our eyes open." He stood to go, handing Ray the cash for their food.

"Afternoon," Bud said as he and Howie walked by the booth. The man nodded his head a bit and smiled, but said nothing.

Ray followed Bud and Howie to the door.

"Thanks for keepin' an eye out for Wanda," he said in a low voice to Howie, then turned to Bud. "And Sheriff, let me know if you see anything suspicious."

Bud nodded, silently groaning. It seemed like everyone was going to keep calling him sheriff, no matter what.

Howie got in the FJ, while Bud casually walked over to the Ford so he could read the emblem on its door. It read, "State of Utah."

It looked to Bud like whatever the guy inside was doing, he was on official business, and Bud couldn't help but wonder if it might have to do with the blue glow Ray had mentioned.

CHAPTER 4

"Sheriff, I've been trying to figure out what's different about you, and now I know. You shaved off your handlebar mustache! Why'd you go and do that? Made you look like an old-time cowboy."

Howie and Bud were bumping in the FJ along the Green River Cutoff, a dirt road that cut across to Castle Dale from the highway between Green River and Price.

"I got tired of the mice trying to eat the crumbs in it every night when I was sleeping," Bud replied. "Wilma Jean would scream every time one ran across her legs and whack me in my sleep."

"You're kidding me," Howie replied incredulously.

"I would never do that," Bud grinned.

The truth was, Wilma Jean had gotten tired of Bud twirling the ends of his mustache. He was always fiddling with something—he couldn't think without fiddling—and she was always trying to figure out how to break him of the habit, so far to no avail. The mustache had worked for quite awhile—until she figured out he wasn't really training it, but fiddling.

This reminded Bud of the clicker in his pocket, but he kept both hands firmly on the steering wheel and managed to not click it. He was trying to quit fiddling, but it was hard.

"What are you going to fiddle with next?" Howie grinned.

"Dunno. I'm thinking about buying a fiddle."

Howie groaned, then said, "Sheriff, Ray back there at the cafe said maybe that guy was an ALF. What's an ALF?"

Bud replied, "An Alien Life Form."

"Oh," Howie replied. "Say, Sheriff, look. There's a rooster tail coming our way."

Someone was indeed coming up the road, Bud noted, and they seemed to be going at a pretty good clip, from the cloud of dust they were raising. A tan car soon appeared in the distance, rocking and tilting as it took the curves and twists of the road.

"I'm gonna stop until he gets by," Bud said, pulling the FJ off the road. "Might be drinking."

The car soon passed them, came to a screeching halt, fishtailing a bit, then backed up until it was next to them. A rough-looking character stared at them from the open window of an old beat-up and rusted Crown Victoria just like Howie's patrol car, but in much worse shape.

The fellow had shoulder-length scraggly hair and wore a pink paisley baseball cap and white t-shirt over a long-sleeved long-johns top that was frayed at the wrists. He appeared to have lost a number of teeth somewhere. Two big brown dogs that looked like German Shepherd mixes sat next to him.

"You fellas have a cell phone?" he asked.

"What's going on?" Bud replied.

"I think we have a missing person case on up the road. I wanna call the sheriff."

"How do you know someone's missing?" Bud asked.

"Because they're not there, that's how."

"I guess that explains that," Bud replied. "The sheriff's already on it." He nodded towards Howie, who looked a bit shocked. Bud knew that Howie had never handled a missing person case.

"Who's missing?" Howie asked, getting out of the FJ.

"Wanda, from down at the cafe."

Howie was now standing over by the car, looking official, as if ready to take notes or interrogate the guy or something, anything to show he was a competent sheriff, Bud suspected. The driver nervously shifted back and forth on his seat, then continued.

"Wanda's cousin called me this morning, said he got a call from her earlier and she was pretty upset, so he and I came out here looking for her, cause I know she rides out here a lot, and we found her horse, but no Wanda. Scrapper, that's her cousin, he's down the road there a bit, bringing her horse back."

Bud couldn't help but notice that the driver was nervous and seemed to avoid eye contact.

"Can I get your name and number?" Howie asked, pulling a little notebook from his shirt pocket. "You have some ID?"

"No, Sheriff, I don't. I'm sorry, I was in such a hurry and so upset I forgot my billfold. My name's Gary Wilder and Ray down at the cafe will vouch for me. I spend a lot of time there hanging out with him and Wanda. Of course, that's when I'm not working, which I usually am, up at the Chevron gas station there in Price. I'm a mechanic, when they have work for me, anyway."

Howie looked at Bud, not sure what to do.

"It's OK, Gary. Happens to the best of us," Bud replied. "The Sheriff of Emery County has better things to do than harass someone who forgot their license. Gary, we're going to head on up the road and see if we can get more info from this guy Scrapper you mentioned. You have a nice day."

Gary looked relieved, and a smile broke across his grizzled face, a face that was wrinkled and lined from too much sun and maybe too much smoking and drinking, Bud thought.

"You boys see if you can figure out what happened—it would be a big relief to find Wanda," Gary said. "I'm guessing it has something to do with them flying saucers everyone's been seeing. Not like her to run off and leave Buck out there. My theory is that she was abducted by a UFO."

Howie was now back in the FJ, and he looked a bit worried. "You think so?" he said in a squeaky voice.

It irritated Bud that Howie was so incredulous, but he tried not to let on. Bud said, "You might want to slow down a bit. Kind of hard on your vehicle, going that fast on these bumps."

"Oh, I will. I was just in a hurry to find the sheriff, but now that I done found him, I'm not so worried."

With that, Gary drove off, though he didn't seem to slow down much, leaving a rooster tail of dust hovering over Bud and Howie like a flying saucer.

"Man, that guy sure seems suspicious," Howie commented.

"Yeah, he does," Bud replied. "But you know, sometimes just talking to the sheriff does that to people, even when they don't have anything to hide, so you can't always put much stock in it."

"Probably true," Howie conceded. "But if Wanda really is missing, he's on my suspect list."

They drove on down the road until they saw a horse in the distance. Bud pulled over and waited, not wanting to spook it.

Howie said, "You know, Sheriff, I'm having a bad day here. I just wasn't sure what to do with that guy back there. He's supposed to be driving with a license, and we just let him get away without having one." He sounded upset.

Bud replied, "It's OK, Howie. I know him. He fixed our old Crown Vic back when I was sheriff, though he didn't act like he remembered me. He must like that model of car, seeing how he's also driving one. Anyway, you have to remember when you're enforcing the law that it was made to protect people, not the other way around."

Bud continued, "My experience has been that guys like that break the law all the time in little ways, like forgetting their license, or maybe not even having a license, drinking too much, all kinds of things, so when they do talk to the law, they're always feeling guilty, even if they haven't done anything much. It's just a general state of being for them. Sometimes that guilt is punishment enough, if you know what I mean. And usually you want them on your side, because they may know something you don't."

"Well," Howie replied. "I didn't want to give him a ticket anyway, especially since he was doing a good deed by looking for Wanda. Like I said, I'm just having a bad day."

"What's going on, Howie, or do you want to talk about it?"

"Not really," Howie answered.

Bud said nothing, watching the horse and rider get closer.

Howie again began drumming his fingers on the dash, then finally said, "It has to do with me and Maureen. You know, ever since we got remarried, things have been great, and this band thing is really something. But she said something last night that really hurt my feelings."

"What was that?" Bud asked gently.

"Well, she said I was stupid."

Bud sighed. It sounded like the honeymoon was over.

"I can't picture Maureen saying something like that to anyone, especially you, Howie."

"Well, she didn't put it exactly like that."

Bud could now see the rider better, and he swore it was Wanda. Whoever it was, they were built just like her, same size, everything.

He waited for Howie to say something. Finally, Howie moaned, "She likes my singing, but sometimes I do things that irritate her. I know that, and I try not to, but I can't just go around singing all the time."

"What exactly did she say, Howie?"

"Well, Sheriff, she said I have a million-dollar voice and a ten-cent brain."

Bud couldn't help but laugh, at which Howie looked put off, but said nothing.

"Howie, that's a compliment. You know who Roy Acuff was?"

"Well, sure, he was the King of Country Music, part of the Grand Ole Opry."

"He once told Hank Williams that same thing. And you know, Hank was one of the old-time greats."

Howie smiled. "He did? You mean Maureen was complimenting me?"

"Sure, that's a compliment, if you ask me. At least half of one, and a really big half—the million dollar half."

Howie said, "Well, I don't know about the million-dollar voice, but I think she's right about the brain. I'm going to try harder not to irritate her."

"Sounds good, Howie."

The rider was now upon them and pulled the big buckskin horse to a stop. Bud would swear it was Wanda, but the day-old stubble on the cheeks said otherwise—it had to be a man.

"Howdy, boys," the rider greeted them in a gruff voice. "You haven't seen a woman around who looks a lot like me and rides a horse just like this one, have you?" With that, the rider tossed them each a cigar.

Bud grinned. He already liked Wanda's cousin, Scrapper.

CHAPTER 5

Scrapper sat on Buck's tall back looking down on Bud and Howie. They were leaning against Bud's FJ, trying to smoke the cigars, but Bud was turning blue and Howie was coughing.

"You boys don't mind if I don't get down, I hope. I'm kinda short, just like Wanda—it runs in the family, and it's hard to get up on this rangy mangy horse. I don't know how she does it."

"She'd be kicking you about now if she heard you call her horse mangy," Howie replied, barely able to talk, a cigar hanging out of his mouth. He then asked with concern, "Where'd you find Buck?"

"He was over by an old trough, back aways, down by the old narrow-gauge railroad grade. He was just standing there like he was ground tied, but I don't think Buck ground ties, so maybe he was thinking about something, like where his next meal was coming from."

Scrapper balanced an unlit cigar in his mouth while talking. His low gruff voice sounded like he smoked cigars all the time, Bud thought, and he was wearing a camo baseball hat with a matching camo jacket, jeans and sneakers, and he had a hand-tooled leather belt with silver studs that had a cell phone holder attached, though there was no phone. The belt also had a leather knife sheath, but no knife. It looked like Scrapper had left home without worrying too much about anything, Bud thought.

"I'm kind of worried about my cousin," Scrapper said, contradicting Bud's theory about him not worrying. "But I sure hate to see you boys get involved. She and Ray got in a big spat, and knowing Wanda, her feelings got hurt. I think she'll probably show up before too long. Maybe she hitched a ride with a friend."

"She would never just leave Buck like that," Bud said. "That horse is her pride and joy, and she would never just walk off without him."

"Oh, I know that," Scrapper replied. "But she brings Buck out here almost every day, and I think she figured he'd just go on home. He probably would have if we hadn't found him first."

Howie looked skeptical. "I don't know...I think maybe it has something to do with UFOs."

"UFOs?" Scrapper asked, incredulous.

Bud knew the way the conversation was turning he might never get back to his irrigating, and besides, it was getting on towards evening and those hopeful meatballs, and he and Howie still needed to check out those coordinates. He needed to turn this conversation around so they could head on down the road.

He interrupted, "Well, Scrapper, we're on our way up the road on some other business, so we need to get going. You OK to get on back to the cafe? Are you staying there overnight or going back home?"

Scrapper answered, "Oh, I'll be staying around for awhile. I'm going to move into Wanda and Ray's spare bedroom. But I'm OK, I can just hang on and let Buck find his way back."

Bud answered, "OK, we need to head on out before it gets too late. Nice meeting you."

He handed what was left of his cigar to Howie and got back into the FJ.

Howie said goodbye to Scrapper, then got in, waited until Scrapper was gone, then threw both cigars out the window.

"Man, Sheriff, that guy was even more suspicious than the first one," Howie commented as they headed on up the road.

"How so?"

"Well, that cigar thing, that was diversionary, meant to throw us off from something, though I don't know what. Sidetrack us."

"Maybe," Bud replied. "But what I found odd was how he seemed unconcerned about Wanda missing. He came out here to look for her, but once he found the horse, he decided she was OK."

"Yeah, that's odd," Howie said. "It was almost like he didn't want us to go looking for her."

"Good point," Bud answered. "It did seem that way."

They continued going west on the Green River Cutoff, and it wasn't long before they had to slow down to cross a wash. About a half-mile later, Bud turned onto a small side track that led north and soon ended by another deep wash that was lined with tamarisk and tall grasses. He pulled the FJ up next to an old rusted-out stock tank and stopped.

"This is where Scrapper said he found Buck. Let's be careful not to step on tracks or anything, Howie. Might be some evidence here," Bud advised.

They got out and began scanning the ground near the tank. Bud walked over to the old railroad grade, the eroded remnant of the days in the late 1800s when the Denver and Rio Grande Railroad tried to build a narrow-gauge line to service the coal mines over around Huntington and Castle Dale. The line didn't get very far because of financial difficulties, and ended just about where Bud was standing.

Howie was now walking around looking for clues, trying to stay on the few clumps of grasses there were, jumping from clump to clump.

"Sheriff!" Howie yelled at Bud. "Over here!"

Bud walked to the clump of grass Howie stood on and looked to where Howie pointed at the ground.

"Horse tracks. And look, they come in from there," Howie pointed towards the road. "They come right up to here and turn around and go right back down the road."

"Good observation, Howie," Bud noted. "But what are you thinking?"

"Well, that horse came in here where they said they found him and just stood as still as can be, waiting to be found, then turned around and left. Didn't mill around or sidestep or anything. And it doesn't look like anyone got on or off him, as there's no people tracks."

"I think you're on to something, Howie," Bud replied. "But why don't you walk around over by the trough a bit and see if there's anything over there, then we probably should get back home."

"What about the coordinates?"

"We're pretty close to them right now, but it's almost dark. We can come back tomorrow." Bud had noticed another rooster tail coming their way, and he'd managed to get a glimpse of the vehicle. It looked to be a white Ford truck.

Howie was now wandering around over by the old stock tank while Bud took a closer look at the horse tracks.

"Whooeee, Sheriff, look at this!" Howie called to Bud.

Bud noted that now the white truck was closer and slowing down—it had obviously spotted them. It pulled off the road behind a rock outcropping where he could no longer see it.

"What'd you find, Howie?"

Howie was holding something in his hand, which he handed to Bud. It was another cigarette paper, just like the one with the coordinates on it, with the words "GI Jay" printed on a camo pattern.

Bud turned it over, but it bore no writing. He'd actually seen it on the ground before Howie did, but figured it would be better for Howie to find it. He'd decided it was time for Howie to solve a crime on his own to boost his self-confidence, so he wouldn't worry so much about having a ten-cent brain.

"This cigarette paper kind of matches Scrapper's jacket and hat." Howie said knowingly.

"It does, but it's also a pretty common brand," Bud replied. "I'd hang onto it, if I were you, but we better get on home."

Bud opened the door of the FJ. He didn't like the fact that they'd been followed, and he wanted to see if the pickup would follow them back.

But suddenly, Howie grabbed Bud's shoulder and whispered, "Sheriff, down there, in the wash!"

Bud looked, but saw nothing out of the ordinary. He stood for a moment, straining to see in the evening light, and while he studied the shadows, he began inadvertently squeezing the clicker.

"Aliens, Sheriff!" Howie whispered again in a kind of panicky squeaky voice. He began scanning the sky above them. "And did you hear that weird electrical clicking noise? It's their spaceship. I bet they kidnapped Wanda, lifted her right off that horse. We better get out of here right now!"

CHAPTER 6

Bud just stood there, squinting, trying to make out what actually did look like several tall dark figures in the wash. Howie was urging him to get in the FJ, but Bud stood, watching. The figures appeared to be shimmering a bit, but didn't move.

Finally, Bud said, "Howie, look a bit closer. Those aren't aliens."

Howie shaded his eyes, staring into the wash. The figures were about a hundred feet away, tall dark shadows along the wash bank.

"Well, they're not moving, Sheriff, but I still think they're aliens. What else could they be? They're too tall and thin to be human, and they're sure not some animal. They're real still cause they're watching us. Let's go."

Bud said, "Howie, look along the top of the bank, right above each shadow."

After awhile, Howie replied, "Hard to see in the glare, but it looks like bushes."

"Exactly. They're casting shadows down into the wash because the sun's so low. The wash is deep enough that the shadows are long and narrow."

Howie stood there for a bit, straining to see, then said in a defeated voice, "Well, I guess you just solved another mystery, Sheriff. My ten-cent brain sure don't think like yours does, that's for sure."

Bud gave Howie's shoulder a pat, then said, "You know, I have lots of experience out in this country, which you don't, Howie. That's all. It's just a matter of knowing what's out here."

"Well, thanks, Sheriff," Howie replied as they got into the FJ. "Maybe I just need more time for my brain to kick in, though you'd think it would have by now, as I ain't no kid. Until then, maybe I should stick to being a musician, cause it sure don't take a lot of brains to play guitar."

"Well, I think you're doing a fine job as sheriff," Bud replied, backing the FJ around and noting the white pickup was now gone—it must have left while he and Howie were looking for aliens.

"Say, Howie, there's a couple of sandwiches in that sack there on the floor. You mind handing me one? The other's for you."

Howie handed Bud the sandwich, then began munching on his.

"Say, Sheriff," Howie said between bites, "I forgot, but I'm supposed to invite you and Wilma Jean to a picnic with me and Maureen down at the state park this evening. Maureen's making up some hamburgers and potato salad. Supposed to be a meteorite shower tonight, so we thought it would be fun to go down there and have a campfire and watch for shooting stars."

"Sounds like fun," Bud said, though he was actually hoping for spaghetti and meatballs. He added, "It might be too late, though, as Wilma Jean's probably got our dinner started."

"No, Maureen already talked to her earlier down at the cafe, so she knows," Howie replied. "Wilma Jean said she's gonna make a lemon-meringue pie."

Maureen had been working for Wilma Jean at the Melon Rind Cafe ever since she came back to Green River from Castle Dale to get back together with Howie.

Bud sighed, then decided the meatballs could wait. He replied, "Sounds like a plan, Howie. What time you guys going down there?"

"Well, let's meet up an hour or so after we get back. That'll give us time to do whatever we need to do, like me getting out of this uniform."

They rode along in silence and soon reached the highway. It was nice to get back on pavement and off the bumpy dirt road.

The sun set over the San Rafael Reef, making the yellow ramparts of Navajo Sandstone glow like hot butter. The fins and whalebacks had been called the Lost City by early settlers and indeed looked like a city of massive rounded buildings and towers.

They soon passed the No Delay Cafe, which, as usual, was empty and forlorn looking way out there by the side of the desert road, at least what they could see of it in the brief moment they went through the dip.

They came to where the highway crossed the railroad tracks on a big sweeping bridge, just as a big freight train came rolling through, and Bud could see the cars beneath them for a moment. It made him think of his Uncle Junior, who had once been a hobo.

"Sheriff," Howie said thoughtfully. "You suppose I'll ever amount to anything as sheriff? Maybe I should take back the drive-in and run that, then do the music on the side. I was pretty happy there, you know, and even though the new owner's kind of getting caught up, he's still three months behind."

Bud answered, "Well, I don't know, Howie. That's something only you can decide, but I think you're doing a fine job as sheriff. A fine job. No need to think otherwise. You can decide when the term's up if you want to continue."

Howie's voice trailed off as the last rays of sunlight faded over the Swell. "Well, I mean, I enjoy it, for the most part, but sometimes I wonder if I'm supposed to be in law enforcement..."

"Who's doin' the supposin', Howie?"

Howie paused, thinking, then replied, "Well, I guess me—well, maybe Maureen."

"You mean she doesn't want you to be sheriff?"

"Oh, I dunno. She's really proud of me, but that remark about the ten-cent brain..."

"Well, she was just repeating what Roy Acuff said. I wouldn't give it too much thought."

Howie relaxed, seeming to take Bud's advice to heart. He started singing, "I'm down to my last wad of chew," then offered Bud a stick of Beeman's gum.

They drove on as the desert gradually took on its mysterious night cloak, that time when most desert creatures come out, avoiding the heat.

Finally, back on the freeway, they could see the lights of the little town of Green River glowing in the distance, out in the middle of what Bud called the Big Empty, that vast expanse of Green River Desert that banked against the white shark's teeth of the San Rafael Reef to the west and rolled on over to the high mesas of Colorado to the east.

The town was flanked to the north by the high ramparts of the Bookcliffs, and to the south a flat sweep of desert stretched out and ended some 50 miles away in the redrock cliffs of the little town of Radium, where Bud had grown up.

Finally back at Bud's bungalow, it was now nearly dark, and they could tell Wilma Jean was home, as her pink Lincoln was parked next to Howie's patrol car.

Howie got out, thanked Bud for the ride, then got into the old Crown Vic and headed back to the Emery County Sheriff's Office, the mysterious letter with the claw forgotten in the afternoon's events and in his anticipation of a picnic at the park.

CHAPTER 7

The Green River State Park was one of those places where, if you didn't know where you were, you would never guess you were in a desert town. It sat on the banks of the Green River and was an oasis with its big grassy lawns and old sheltering cottonwoods.

The park was bordered by an eight-hole golf course, which added to the surreal feel one got when gazing out and seeing the expanse of Mancos shale just on the other side of the river. But the desert likewise added to the sheltering feel of the park by making one appreciate all the green, and it was a popular place for travelers and locals alike.

Bud and Wilma Jean pulled up next to Howie and Maureen's shiny blue VW Bug, which was parked at one of the camp spots in the park. The couple had already started a fire in the fire pit, and Howie was watching over a grill holding hamburgers wrapped in aluminum foil.

Hoppie and Pierre jumped out of the car and ran over to Howie, where they wagged their tales and wiggled around, hoping to convince him they were good dogs deserving of hamburger.

The park wasn't too busy, but they were next to a camp site reserved for large parties, and Bud noted that is was occupied by a group whose cars had Colorado license plates. There were a half-dozen or so tents and the group was sitting around a campfire, talking and enjoying dinner.

The burgers soon done, Bud and everyone sat and ate, enjoying the smell of smoke and the night sky above. It reminded Bud of the many times he'd camped in this country and down around Radium and the carefree feeling it always gave him.

After dinner, Howie pulled out his guitar, and they all sat around the fire as he strummed some tunes. He hadn't been playing for very long, but Bud noted he seemed to be picking it up pretty quickly and wasn't half-bad.

"You've gotten really good on that thing fast," Bud said.

"Thanks, Sheriff," Howie replied.

"All he does is practice," Maureen smiled. "He has a lot of natural talent."

"It's about all I can do with my ten-cent brain and all," Howie said glumly.

Maureen laughed, then said in a more serious tone, "Sweetie, you're never going to forget I said that, are you? I told you I was just kidding. It's almost like you just want to believe it."

Howie didn't reply and started strumming the old Hank Williams' song, "I'm So Lonesome I Could Die." The look on his face went with the song, Bud thought.

Hoppie and Pierre, their tummies full of hamburger, snuggled down next to Wilma Jean, where she and Bud sat on a blanket on the grass.

Howie now stopped playing and said, "Hey, you wanna hear a song I just wrote? When I was a kid, I thought you pronounced the name 'Tucson' like 'Tuckson.' I didn't know the 'c' was silent. So, I made up a little song about it."

Howie started singing:
I'm just a young Texan from Tuckson,
Drivin' my Mercedes Benz.
I'm just a young Texan from Tuckson,
Tuckson where the fun never ends.
But I'd rather be out in the desert,
Listenin' to coyotes and wrens.
I'd rather be out in the desert,
Where the sun always shines through the winds.

Howie sat his guitar down as everyone started clapping, looking embarrassed.

As the night breeze stirred, they all grew quiet, leaning a bit closer to the fire and silently watching the embers glow.

In contrast, the group next to them seemed to have perked up and were now getting a bit boisterous.

"Here's how you do it," said someone with a deep raspy voice. "You put the butter, sugar, and spices in your mug, mix it all up, or muddle it, then you add the rum."

All was quiet as the speaker demonstrated.

"Then you take this poker here out of the fire, be real careful, and you stick it in the mug. See, the red-hot poker caramelizes everything. Hold it in there for about one minute, but be careful not to touch the glass, or it'll shatter. Woila, hot buttered rum!"

Just then, as if on cue, Bud could hear the sound of shattering glass. He and Wilma Jean looked at each other knowingly, while Maureen tried not to laugh.

Now Howie whispered to Bud, "Sheriff, is it legal to drink like that here in the park?"

"Probably not, Howie," Bud replied, wondering what Howie would do.

Maureen jabbed Howie gently in the ribs. "They're not hurting anything. Let them have their fun."

Howie answered sheepishly, "I wasn't gonna arrest any-body, Maureen, I just wondered if it was legal—for future reference, you know, in case I'm patrolling through here and see a wild drunken brawl going on, tearing the place up, or something like that."

Bud replied, "Well, Sheriff, I never patrolled the state park, I just let the on-duty ranger take care of things. Seemed to work out OK."

Howie looked relieved. "I wasn't interested in arresting anybody, that's for sure." He gave Maureen a look that said he felt a bit persecuted, then added, "Besides, I don't even have a jail. I'd have to take them clear over to the court-house in Castle Dale."

Wilma Jean turned her head towards Bud so Howie couldn't see her big smile. She was trying hard not to laugh.

Now the group was talking louder and louder.

A woman's voice said, "You know, we need to go out to the No Delay Cafe early tomorrow and see if we can figure out what's going on, so everyone needs to get some rest tonight. Don't party too hearty."

Bud wondered what interest the group had in the cafe, but his question was soon answered.

A man said, "Yeah, that post on our website this morn-ing about the woman being abducted by a UFO out there sounds like a hot lead."

Bud groaned, and Howie commented, "That's all we need while we're trying to find Wanda, Sheriff, is a bunch of UFO crazies. You suppose that's what they are, right?"

Maureen replied, "They sound like some kind of organized group, having a webpage and all. I wonder where they're from."

"Some place in Colorado," Howie said. "They have Colorado plates. Probably Grand Junction, since it's not very far."

"I bet Ray posted it. Maybe he's hoping the more eyes the better for finding Wanda," Wilma Jean said. "And maybe he's right. Or maybe he's trying to drum up more business, since the cafe's dying off."

"The cafe's in a bad spot, there in that dip," Bud added. "Can't see it until you're right on it, and there's no turn lane, so people just whiz on by."

Now the campers began talking even louder.

One said, "There's other life forms out there in the universe, you know, we humans ain't alone. The universe is so big that we can't even begin to see what's out there, even with the Hubble."

Someone replied, "Yeah, and it's getting bigger all the time, expanding, what with the Big Bang and all."

Another said, "And governments around the globe are trying to cover up the fact that we're not alone. Sooner or later, somebody's gonna spill the beans."

Someone else answered, "I personally welcome new life forms to earth. We need more diversity. If they could just quit crashing and having their bodies confiscated, they might eventually make some progress here."

Now a new voice spoke, and after listening, Bud figured she must be the skeptic in the group.

"Right. These aliens, who can move from galaxy to galaxy and are supposedly so much more advanced—why would a species so advanced always be involved in crashes and near collisions? I'll tell you, if these are the best the aliens have for flying craft, we don't have anything to worry about if they attack someday."

"Aw, Lillian, I don't know why you even come along, since you don't believe in nuthin'," someone said.

Lillian ignored the comment and continued, "All we have to do is send out some drones and let them fly around randomly and the aliens will just crash into them, given the amount of near-misses reported in the past few decades. No problem, not a threat at all."

One of the previous voices said, "You know that new video that just came out? That one in Denver the guy shot of that round blue thing glowing and hovering above the state capitol? I just heard that the Turkish government studied the footage and came away with the conclusion that it's not a hoax."

Now Lillian laughed, "The Turkish government? Ha! Ha! Ha! You've got rocks for brains." She then continued, "I can't imagine what it would be like on these aliens' planet, because they would be crashing all the time and running into each other. Your argument that they're advanced is crazy. They're a bunch of bumbling dumb-asses."

Someone replied, "And you got this wisdom broadcast through your tooth fillings, right, Lillian?"

Bud and Wilma Jean looked at each other and started laughing. Wanda was also smiling, but Howie looked a bit perturbed.

Now somebody was yelling, "Attention all planets of the Solar Federation! Attention all planets of the Solar Federation! We have assumed control!"

"Shut up, Dewey," another voice yelled. "You're gonna get us in trouble."

Dewey continued yelling, "The truth is out there! We have found it! It has been erased!"

"Would you just shut up already, Dewey?" another voice pleaded.

"Yeah, Dewey," Lillian said sarcastically. "Don't you know the Prime Directive of the United Federation of Planets forbids interference with pre-warp societies?"

Dewey now continued, but in a quieter voice, "Ancient aliens are in the Bible—you know, Ezekiel saw a wheel way up in the middle of the air and all that."

Lillian said, "Yeah, but no big deal. Even baseball is in the Bible. The first four words: 'In the big inning.'"

Bud started laughing out loud while inadvertently squeezing the dog-training clicker in his pocket.

Just then, the sky parted as a huge glowing orb of light cut through the clouds, leaving a green phosphorescent streak behind. It was soon followed by a loud boom that echoed off the distant Bookcliffs, then back to where they all sat.

"It's a UFO!" Howie shouted, jumping to his feet. "It had that same weird electrical clicking noise I heard earlier, and it's crashed right out of town!"

CHAPTER 8

Howie was now standing on his tiptoes on top of a picnic table, trying to see if he could make out any signs of an alien craft crashed in the desert, about ready to crash himself as the table wobbled back and forth.

"See anything?" Bud asked. "Any strange glow or smaller ships taking off from the mother ship or anything like that?"

"No," Howie said, obviously disappointed, finally climbing back down. "It probably put up its invisible shields or something so nobody can see it—I dunno, or something."

Now the group next to them were in their cars, apparently to go look for aliens. This worried Bud.

"That bunch has been drinking, and I don't think it's a good idea for them to be out driving," he said.

"Dang it, Sheriff," Howie said with concern, "Do you think I should go home and get into my uniform and get the patrol car?"

"They'll be long gone by then, Howie."

Bud wanted to tell Howie what he thought he should do, but since Maureen was there, he figured it would be better for Howie to figure it out himself. It would make Howie look more professional.

"Well dagnabit," Howie fussed, then started walking in a circle around the picnic table as if thinking. Bud wondered if Howie might be a candidate for developing a fiddling habit like his own.

"Well, I know what to do," Howie finally said, after a couple of rounds. "I'll call the State Troopers and give them a heads up. Those kids will soon be out on the freeway anyway, and that's more their jurisdiction."

"Good thinking, Howie," Bud replied. "I'm not sure I would've thought of that."

Wilma Jean gave him a puzzled look, but Maureen didn't notice, as she was now busy picking up the picnic stuff as she said to Howie, "Let's go on home, Sweetie. It's sure been fun, you guys." She smiled at Bud and Wilma Jean.

"Well," Howie replied, "I was kinda hoping to go on out and see if we could find that UFO."

Bud said, "Howie, I'd stake my life on that being a meteorite. You might be able to find something tomorrow, but not tonight in the dark. There won't be a glow or anything, and who knows where it hit. I kind of think it exploded, from the sounds of it, so it probably vaporized."

Howie looked disappointed. "A meteorite?"

"Well, yeah, aren't you the one who said tonight was a meteor shower?"

"Oh, yeah, I forgot all about that," Howie answered, sighing. "It's the Eta Aquariids. They're associated with Halley's Comet, and tonight's the peak. Their radiant is in Aquarius, and Eta Aquarii is the constellation's brightest star, but it's way down on the horizon at this time of year, so they're not as visible as some, say the Leonids or Geminids."

He gently turned Maureen by her shoulder and pointed to the horizon. "See that big white star right there by that tree limb? That's Eta Aquaarii."

Just then, a small streak of blue shot across the sky, fading into the distant ramparts of the San Rafael Reef.

Maureen took Howie's hand and squeezed it. "Not bad for a ten-cent brain," she laughed. "Sweetie, where did you learn so much about astronomy? And how can you believe in aliens knowing all that?"

Howie suddenly seemed embarrassed. "Dunno. Just something I've liked since I was a kid. Not much else to do in Sunnyside at night. And it is possible there are aliens out there, it's a big universe. It's not completely out of the question, you know."

"I didn't know you grew up in Sunnyside," Bud replied. "Was your dad a coal miner?"

"Not my dad, my mom," Howie replied. "She worked for the mines in the office there. My dad was the postman. But hey, I forgot..."

Howie now pulled out his cell phone and called the Utah Highway Patrol in Green River, explaining the situation, while Bud and Wilma Jean packed up their picnic stuff, getting Hoppie and Pierre into the car.

When Howie finished the call, he turned to Maureen and took her hand, saying, "Wanna go out looking for aliens with me?"

Bud could see her smile in the glow of the fire's last embers.

"Sure," she replied, like a teen being asked to the prom.

Howie grinned and squeezed her hand.

"Sheriff," he said. "Me and my wife are gonna go see if we can find that thing. Where do you suppose the best place would be to start looking?"

"Well," Bud replied, "It kind of looked like it might have gone over above the Cutoff Road, but distances can be deceiving. Do you have a good flashlight and a magnet?"

"A magnet?" asked Wilma Jean.

"Yeah, meteorites are typically mostly iron," Bud replied.

"Good idea, Sheriff," Howie said. "I actually have one in the office I use for a paperweight. It came out of some old speakers I had. We'll stop by and get it."

"Howie, you know the odds of finding anything are extremely rare," Bud said as Wilma Jean poked him in the ribs. "But you never know," he added.

With that, he and Wilma Jean got into her Lincoln, and she backed the car around. Bud could see Howie and Maureen in the rearview mirror, standing by the picnic table, looking at the night sky, arms around each other's waists.

"Maybe the honeymoon's not over after all," he said to Wilma Jean.

"What, Hon?" she replied absentmindedly.

"Never mind," Bud replied, smiling to himself as they drove on home, the dogs asleep between them on the front seat, probably dreaming of chasing alien rabbits, Bud thought.

CHAPTER 9

Bud once again stood in the irrigation ditch out at Krider's melon farm, waiting for the head of water to arrive. As with the previous day, he'd also once again forgotten his irrigating boots—but today he had a good excuse.

He was still trying to digest the bad news Wilma Jean had fed him at breakfast this morning—the news that she and Maureen had decided to become vegetarians, which, since they did most of the cooking, meant he and Howie would also become vegetarians.

She had tried to console him after he told her he might as well just die now and get it over with. Vegetarianism, explained Wilma Jean, was healthier and would also help her lose the few pounds she'd been working on over the winter, and she was also sure Bud would soon lose his extra weight, too, especially since it seemed men lost weight easier than women.

Bud didn't really mind if Wilma Jean started eating more vegetables, but what he did mind was the part of the deal where she would no longer be cooking the kinds of dinners Bud liked—creamy gravies and meat and potatoes.

"Aren't potatoes vegetables?" Bud had asked, to which she had replied, "Yes, but the wrong kind of vegetables—too starchy."

From now on, their meals would consist of salads and fruits and very few breads or carbohydrates—and lots of hummus, whatever the heck that was. Bud had groaned.

He'd been looking forward to Wilma Jean making those meatballs tonight, the ones he'd wanted last night before he knew they were going on a picnic with Howie and Maureen.

He felt a bit petulant, like a kid—if he'd known what was coming down the pike, he would've definitely held out for handmade meatballs, not lowly every-day hamburgers.

Once again, the water arrived down the ditch without him noticing, washing up over his boots and seeping into the lace holes, this time getting his feet wet. He needed to get a can of SnoSeal and re-waterproof the boots, he thought.

Continuing the replay of the day before, Bud's cell phone rang, and he pulled it from his shirt pocket as he stepped from the water and up onto the ditch bank. He somehow knew it would be Howie.

"Yell-ow," he said distractedly, shaking water from his boots.

"Sheriff, it's Howie. You got time to go out with me again and see if we can figure out those coordinates?"

"Sure, Howie," Bud replied. "I just set the water, so I'm free as of right now."

"Roger," Howie replied. "I'll be right over. You want me to bring a couple of sandwiches?"

"That would be great," Bud answered, grinning. Howie was a good sandwich maker, and maybe it would help Bud head off his inevitable starvation for a few hours.

Bud continued, "Meet me at the house. I'm heading out right now."

"10-4," Howie said, hanging up the phone.

Bud threw his irrigation shovel into the back of the farm truck and headed for the bungalow. He would make a thermos of coffee and grab a few things, including his Ruger, and he and Howie could go see where things led them.

Hopefully they could solve the mystery of the dinosaur claw and enjoy a little rock hounding in the process. Bud always loved getting out in the back country and kicking around.

As he opened the kitchen door, sure enough, Hoppie barked his fool head off while Pierre waited behind the corner, then attacked Bud's pant leg, dragging along as Bud made his way to the refrigerator.

Bud took out a small piece of leftover ham and split it, tossing it to the dogs, Pierre letting go of Bud's pant leg.

It was becoming a form of extortion, he thought, the dogs colluding to get goodies, waiting for him to come in and then barking and Pierre grabbing his pant leg, not letting go until Bud gave them a treat.

He started the coffeepot, grabbed his gun, the atlas, and his jacket, and then looked again in the fridge.

He was hoping there would be something good in there for a snack, like maybe a piece of apple pie, but all that he could find was a big plastic container with a lid on it. He opened it to find it was filled with something that reminded him vaguely of alfalfa.

Now he noticed the crockpot was turned on and there was a note next to it. He lifted the lid and noted a nice pot roast cooking. Maybe his wife was going to have mercy on him after all and cook him stuff he liked while she ate the alfalfa. He then read the note:

"Hon, turn crockpot to low when you get home. It's for the kids for dinner. XXOO"

Bud felt a bit slighted. Wilma Jean was making pot roast for the dogs, and he just knew she was going to make him eat whatever was in that bowl.

Oh well, he sighed, he wouldn't last long on that stuff, so at least his demise would be quick. Maybe he could sneak some meals down at Wilma Jean's cafe, the Melon Rind, when she was bowling, or maybe he could get Howie to make him an occasional sandwich.

Just as Bud was pouring coffee into his thermos, he heard Howie drive up. He looked out the window, noting that Howie had the Toyota Land Cruiser, so the repair must be finished. This was good, as Bud needed to put gas in his FJ, and this would save them the stop.

Bud took a carton of vanilla bean ice cream from the freezer and put a couple of dollops into the thermos, then added the hot coffee.

He grinned, feeling clever—this was his own redneck version of a latte, and to heck with the diet, a man had to enjoy life once in awhile. He then panicked a bit, wondering if the ice cream would also become off limits. He added a third dollop just in case, then screwed on the lid, grabbed a couple of mugs and headed out the door.

Howie handed Bud a pastrami sandwich as he got into the Land Cruiser. Bud unwrapped it and took a big bite, noting it was made on a light rye bread with melted cheese and a bit of sauerkraut and mustard, with sweet pickles, barbecue chips, and deep-fried onions crammed on top. Bud felt better after the first bite, rethinking his being miffed at Howie over the meatballs.

Howie's drive-in had been the best place in town for sandwiches before Howie sold it, and he truly had a knack for putting things together in unique and tasty ways. Too bad the current owner was running it into the ground, Bud thought, thinking he otherwise could've just eaten there until Wilma Jean came to her senses.

"Did you guys find any aliens last night?" Bud asked through a mouthful as Howie backed out and got onto King's Lane, heading into town.

"Maybe," Howie replied. He seemed unusually serious. "Open that pack on the seat behind you."

Bud turned and grabbed the pack. It was heavy, and he had a hunch what was in it. Sure enough, it held a large chunk of a very heavy black rock, one that was shiny and pocked with tiny holes.

"How in hellsbells did you guys manage to find this?" he asked incredulously. "If this is the real deal, it's worth a fortune, Howie."

"Oh, it's the real deal alright," Howie said. "Totally magnetic. We found it exactly where you said to look, out on the Cutoff Road. There might've been more meteorites there, but we chickened out and left."

"Why was that?"

"Bud, you won't believe me, but I have Maureen as my witness. I don't want to go back out there, but I guess we have to." He paused.

Finally, Bud asked, "Witness to what?"

"A real live alien, Bud. It came right over to where we were looking around with the flashlight, not more than 20 feet away from us. It had a strange blue glow around it. It was kind of short and had white antennae, all curled up over its head. It was menacing looking. I swear it was real, Sheriff, as real as that sandwich you're eating. We didn't stick around to talk to it, assuming it even spoke English."

Bud whistled a long low whistle, then said, "I'll be danged. A real live alien? Well, I guess you'll have to tell me more about it."

CHAPTER 10

"Howie, are you sure it was an actual being and not an optical illusion, like the aliens we saw in the wash?" Bud asked, as he poured Howie a cup of coffee. They were nearing the No Delay Cafe but weren't going to stop, since they already had sandwiches and coffee.

"No, Sheriff, I know what you're thinking, but you'll just have to talk to Maureen. It wasn't no optical illusion. It was as real as you and me."

"Where were you guys?" Bud handed Howie the cup, then poured himself one.

"It was hard to tell in the dark, but we were somewhere not too far from that stock tank where Wanda disappeared. I think it's all related, Bud. I'd like to stop there and look around some more. Might find another meteorite."

Bud replied, "Well, if that's a real meteorite, it's probably worth a few thousand dollars."

"It's the real deal, alright, Sheriff," Howie said, sipping the hot coffee. "Say, this is good stuff. Really creamy."

"Secret recipe," Bud replied. "But are you sure it's a real meteorite?"

"Yup. My dad was like you—he loved to rock hound, and every spring my parents would take us kids to the

Tucson Gem and Mineral Show. I've seen lots of meteorites down there. There's always guys selling them."

They were now cruising by the cafe. Since it sat in a dip, they only saw it for a moment, and it was soon again out of sight.

Howie noted, "Man, that place is full today! Did you see all the cars?"

"It looked to me like the Colorado UFOers," Bud replied. "I guess they didn't get in trouble last night."

"Yeah," Howie said. "We were listening to the radio on our way and didn't hear any state patrol chatter."

"You had the Land Cruiser?" Bud asked.

"Yeah, no way could we get out there in Maureen's VW Bug. I figured if anything weird was going on in the county, it was official business."

"Right," Bud answered. They had now turned off the highway onto the Green River Cutoff.

"Say, Sheriff..." Howie said, his voice trailing off.

Bud waited for him to continue, but he didn't. They were now crossing the railroad tracks, and Bud could see the tail end of a train in the distance, on its way to Price.

"Too bad we missed that train," he said, thinking of the Canon camera in his pack. "Could've got some nice shots with Mt. Elliot in the background."

"You're doing really well with that thing, aren't you?" Howie commented. "Wilma Jean said you're in a show up in Price."

Bud swallowed hard. This was news to him, and he wasn't sure if this was a good thing or not. Ever since his wife had bought him the camera, he'd been really enjoying getting out and taking photos, with trains being his main interest.

Since Green River was on the main track between Denver and Salt Lake City, he had lots of opportunities to take train photos. The engineers were even beginning to recognize him and would honk the big horns when they saw him. He had a fantasy of riding on one of the engines someday and blowing the whistle himself.

Now Howie continued with his train of thought. "Sheriff, is Wilma Jean doing to you what Maureen is to me? It's inhumane."

Bud wasn't sure exactly what Howie was referring to, and said so.

"You know, making you eat like a rabbit."

Bud laughed. "Yup. I figure I've got maybe a couple of months left to live is all. That's about how much extra fat I've got."

Howie replied, "Well, I'm already too skinny, so I may only have a week or so. I guess they'll figure it out when we're dead and gone, but in the meantime, it's just plain torture."

Bud agreed, and Howie added, "Maybe I should stock up on sandwich supplies there at the office. You can come down and have lunch with me every day. The county would be in dire straits if we were both gone, so we can consider it for national defense, or county security, or something like that."

Bud replied, "I think that's a great idea, Howie. I'll pay for my share, or even your share too, since you're making them."

"Nah, I'll cover it, Bud. You can keep giving me free advice in exchange."

Bud finished his coffee, then said, "Don't look now, Howie, but that same white pickup's behind us. You know, the state one."

"Is he following us?" Howie asked.

"Well, yes, in the sense that he's behind us," Bud replied. "I don't know if he's actually interested in what we're doing or not, though."

They drove on a bit, Bud wondering what the guy in the pickup was up to, until Bud could see a horse and rider ahead, coming down the side of the road. It looked like Wanda and Buck. Howie slowed down, and Bud noted the pickup behind them did the same.

They finally reached the rider and stopped. It wasn't Wanda, but rather Scrapper. Bud now noticed the white truck had pulled over as if waiting, not wanting to pass them by.

"Well, howdy there, boys," Scrapper said in his gravelly voice, a cigar hanging from his mouth. "Fine mornin', ain't it?"

"Mornin'," Bud replied, his arm resting on the window.

"You want a cigar?" asked Scrapper.

"Oh, no thanks, but thanks a lot. Just had some coffee," Bud said, while Howie nodded in agreement. "Anything goin' on out here?"

"Nope, just out exercisin' the horse and lookin' for my cousin. You boys put out an APB yet for her bein' missin'?"

"Not yet," Bud said. Something just wasn't right about this character, he thought, but he couldn't put his finger on it.

"Well, you might wanna hold off on that anyway," Scrapper replied. "We got this bunch from over in Colorado, and they're gonna go lookin'."

"A bunch from Colorado?" asked Howie. "Would that be that UFO bunch?"

Scrapper looked surprised. "How do you know about them?"

"Oh, we saw them down at the state park last night," Howie said. "You know, Scrapper, having a bunch of yahoos out here wandering around might get in the way, mess up the evidence and all that."

Scrapper replied, "Oh, Sheriff, not to worry, there's so much country out here they could wander around for years and not mess up nuthin'. They'll be careful." He flicked the ashes off his cigar, then continued, "Well, gotta run. You boys take care. Say, you out here lookin' for Wanda by any chance?" He seemed unconcerned.

Bud answered, "Not officially. We're here on other business, but I can assure you we're keeping an eye out for her."

Scrapper replied, "Well, you boys be careful. We had reports last night of another flyin' saucer. Who knows what's going on, but it sure is spookin' me."

Scrapper said goodbye and rode on down the road. Howie started the Land Cruiser and headed out.

"I dunno, Sheriff, but there sure is something suspicious about that guy," Howie said.

Bud agreed that there indeed was, while noting that the pickup was again following them.

"And Sheriff," continued Howie, "Just what's an APB, anyway?"

Bud grinned. "That's an All Points Bulletin, Sheriff. Something you might probably want to remember."

Howie looked a bit sheepish as he turned in and parked by the old stock tank.

CHAPTER 11

"Where exactly did you find the meteorite, Howie?" Bud asked.

Howie was wandering around, looking at the ground. Finally, he replied, "Over here, Sheriff. It was on the ground here, right by these tracks."

"Tracks?" Bud responded. "Buck's?"

"No, these different ones. But Sheriff, I been thinking, and I know why Ray kept hanging up the phone."

"Why's that, Howie?"

Howie continued walking around, scanning the ground. He finally replied, turning a small rock over with his foot. "He was hoping you'd answer the phone. He wanted to talk to you because he thinks I'm incompetent."

Bud sighed. "No, Howie, he thought I was still the sheriff, that's all."

"Well, Bud, that's nice of you to try not to hurt my feelings, but why wouldn't he want to talk to me, even if he thought you were still sheriff? I'm a lawman, too."

Bud answered, "I dunno. Some people are just like that, especially with something they consider important, like their wife missing. They want to go straight to the top. It doesn't mean he thinks you're incompetent. But show me these other tracks, Howie."

Howie led Bud over behind the stock tank a ways, pointing to the ground. "Here."

Bud bent over, examining the tracks. They were small and cloven, like a calf's.

Now Howie sounded upset and nervous. "Bud, this is where we saw that alien, and I'm starting to feel spooked. I'd kinda like to get out of here. See these cloven hoof-prints? I think they're the alien's, and you can see for yourself we didn't hallucinate it."

Howie pulled a little digital camera from his pocket and started taking pictures. Bud recognized that camera. He'd used it himself when he was sheriff, before Wilma Jean had bought him his nice Canon SLR.

Howie continued, "And I think it's related to that claw, Sheriff. See, cloven prints and claws—maybe it's like I said before, some kind of weird devil worship thing."

Bud tried not to laugh. "Howie, these are bighorn sheep prints. Lots of sheep here on the Swell, though they're usually more up in the rocks."

He nodded to the nearby slopes of Cedar Mountain behind them, then said. "They're more up there or out on the Wedge and down in the canyons."

Howie looked suspicious. "Are you sure? They look too small."

"No, Howie, they're definitely bighorn. I've seen plenty of prints. You go over by Drowned Hole Draw and you'll see lots of them. There's wild burros out here, too, and they have the same type of prints, though a bit bigger. And look, here's your and Maureen's tracks, right about 20 feet from the bighorn tracks."

Bud paused, not wanting to upset Howie, then said gently, "You don't suppose that's what you guys saw last night, do you? Probably a young buck kicked out of the herd by the main buck. It's kind of odd that it would come up so close, but I betcha it was curious, seeing people out at night with lights and all. Maybe it thought you were aliens."

Howie said nothing, just turned and continued looking at the tracks. Bud tried not to smile, but couldn't help himself.

Now, an airplane crested out over Cedar Mountain above them, the sound suddenly filling the air. It looked to be a Cessna, maybe a Piper Cub, and Bud wondered why it was flying so low. Probably one of the guys up at Redtail Aviation in Price giving some tourists a tour of the Swell.

Now Bud noted the white truck was parked down the road a bit, just sitting. He didn't like this one bit, and was beginning to wonder what was going on. Only one way to really know, he thought—go ask.

"Howie, we can come back another time and look for meteorites. I still think you just got lucky and found an old one. You saw all those pit marks? It looked a bit eroded to me. But anyway, we need to get on going and do what we came out here for, find those coordinates."

They got into the Land Cruiser, Howie saying nary a word.

Bud added, "I think we need to go over to that pickup and see what he's doing following us."

Howie looked surprised, then said, "You sure about that, Sheriff? Maybe we'd be better off letting him reveal himself more. He'd probably lie to us, anyway."

"You're right, Howie," Bud replied, though he thought otherwise. He was a straightforward kind of guy and thought it best to just go ask, but he wanted Howie to be the lead on this case, so he deferred.

They drove on up the road, the white pickup now again following. Howie seemed a bit sullen, and they rode along in silence for awhile.

Finally, Howie said, "You know, Sheriff, I know all about bighorn sheep. We have lots of them up at Sunnyside. They come down out of Whitmore Canyon, and people even go for drives up there sightseeing for them. There's an old man living there on the edge of town, and usually the creek dries up by the end of summer, especially since they put in Grassy Trail Reservoir, and he puts water out for them in stock tanks. I used to see them every day. I can't believe we thought that was an alien. It was a lot shorter than an alien should be, and I just figured they'd adapted so they could fly smaller crafts and use less fuel between stars, since it's so far."

Bud replied, "Well, Howie, no honor lost there. It's called the power of suggestion, and it's an old survival tactic employed by the human brain. See, you have something in mind, and you're all primed to see it. That's why people who belong to UFO clubs see lots more UFOs than the average bear."

Howie nodded, and Bud could tell he felt a bit better.

"Want another cup of coffee?" Bud asked.

"Sure," Howie answered.

Bud poured him a cup, then another for himself.

"Turn right about a quarter mile," Bud said. "There's a little two-track going up into a draw. I think those coordinates are right up there on that ridge." Bud pointed to a cliff above the road to the right about a half mile.

"You been here before?" Howie asked.

"Yup," Bud answered. "I used to come out here a lot before me and Wilma Jean got married. Tourist season in

Radium gets pretty crazy, so I'd come up here to get away from everybody, go rockhounding."

He sipped his coffee, then said, "You know, Howie, that pickup's still following us. I'm wondering if it doesn't have something to do with those coordinates. Maybe somebody wants to know something we know, even though we don't know it yet. Maybe we should just keep going instead of giving it away. We can come back in from the other side and ditch that pickup."

"The other side?"

"Yeah. Let's drive on over to Elmo and visit Larry—you remember him from up at the Ghost Rock Cafe. He has a little hay farm there. Then we can come back and hopefully the guy in the pickup will have given up by then."

"Does this road go to Elmo?"

"Yes, in a way. It actually goes on over to Castle Dale, but there's a spur that goes on up to Elmo and then comes out at Price."

They drove on, passing the turnoff that led to where Bud thought the coordinates were, the pickup still following. The plane they'd spotted earlier had circled back over them, losing a bit of altitude.

It wasn't long before they took a right off the main Cut-off Road and climbed up out of the lower country, going east, towards Elmo.

"I have cell service now," Bud said. "I'll see if Larry's home." He dialed a number.

"Hello," a voice answered. Bud could hear road noise in the background, like the engine of a big truck.

"Larry, Bud here. We're not too far from your place. You home and want some company?"

"Well, shoots," Larry said. "Nope, I'm working today, dang it."

"You still doing long hauls for Dyno-Noble?" Bud asked.

"No, Bud, I'm working up here for the Sunnyside Mine, hauling coal down to the power plant by Helper. Got tired of never being home. I sure hate that I missed you, though."

Bud and Howie were now passing a turnoff road with a sign that read, "Cleveland-Lloyd Dinosaur Quarry." Bud could now see that the white pickup had turned off onto that road and was continuing on down towards the quarry, which was a few miles on into the candy-cane striped hills of the Brushy Basin Member of the Morrison Formation.

The quarry contained the densest concentration of Jurassic-aged dinosaur bones ever found, with over 12,000 bones having been excavated to date. Bud and Wilma Jean had visited it a couple of times, taking the hike down to the building that set over the quarry itself, protecting it from the elements and dino-bone thieves.

Bud could now see the Cessna plane coming back around their way, and he wondered once again what it was doing. He noted that it was sure flying low.

"Well, Larry," Bud said. "You come on down sometime and we'll feed you dinner."

"Thanks, Bud. But I'm wondering if you got my invite to the..." But the cell phone connection was gone.

Bud hung up, not sure in retrospect if inviting Larry down was such a good idea or not, as he suspected Larry wouldn't like rabbit food any more than he and Howie did. He wondered what Larry was trying to tell him. An invitation? Must be to the Elk's Club Friday night dinner up there in Price, as Larry had invited him before, but Bud was usually too busy to go.

"Sheriff," Howie said. "That pickup's gone. Should we turn back now?"

"Might as well," Bud replied as Howie stopped and began turning the Land Cruiser around.

"That is, if you can," Bud added, ducking, as he could now see the landing gear of the Cessna just above the Land Cruiser's front window.

It soon landed right smack on the road in front of them, one wheel bouncing up in the air a bit, then settling down and stopping, a cloud of dust coming in through Bud's open window.

"Holy smokes!" Howie exclaimed, bringing the Land Cruiser to a sudden stop, skidding on the dirt a bit.

"That was close!" Bud added.

THE NO DELAY CAFE

CHAPTER 12

"Just my luck to nearly land on top of a sheriff's vehicle," said the pilot of the Cessna. He'd climbed out of the plane and was now eyeing the Land Cruiser.

He was white as a sheet and rubbing his bald head distractedly. Bud wondered how he fit into the small plane, as he was a really big guy.

"Sheriff, I'm Cherokee Smith."

The man held out his hand to Howie, who shook it, whereupon the man continued.

"I fly out of Salt Lake City with Cherokee Flights. I sure do apologize for probably scaring the bejeebers out of you fellows, but I'm having fuel problems, probably a clogged line, and the engine kept cutting out, so I scoped it out and decided to land on the road here, since you were the only traffic."

He stopped to take a breath, obviously shaken, then continued again.

"I wanted to try and catch you guys so I wouldn't be stranded out here all alone, but I didn't anticipate you turning around just as I was coming down. That was about as close a call as I've ever had, and I flew a bush plane in Alaska for 25 years."

Howie's face had now turned from white to red, and Bud wondered what he was going to do next.

Cherokee Smith must have wondered, too, as he said to Howie, "Sheriff, it's not illegal to land on a road if you're having an emergency. In fact, in Alaska, vehicles have to give landing airplanes the right of way on highways."

Howie finally spoke, a bit discombobulated. Bud noted he hadn't looked to him for advice, which was a first.

"I dunno, Mr. Cherokee. I just don't know if Utah says this is legal or not. I would kind of guess generally not, but since it's an emergency, I dunno."

Cherokee now relaxed a bit and said, "The FAA says it's OK, no prohibitions, but it's also my understanding that all state or local laws are waived in an emergency. Rule 91.3. The FAA usually will investigate it, though, and they can cite you for being reckless, but in this kind of deal, that never happens. See, I'm a superior pilot, and the superior pilot usually exercises his superior judgment to avoid exercising his superior skill, but once in awhile you have no choice but to exercise that skill, like today."

Bud was now guessing this wasn't the first time Cherokee Smith had landed on a road, especially since he could cite the rule saying it was legal.

Bud now asked, "Say, we saw you flying around and figured you were out of Price, sightseeing, but that doesn't appear to be the case." He hoped the guy would offer what he was up to.

Cherokee said, "No, I'm just out doing some recon for a client." He then buttoned up, pretty much ignoring Bud.

Howie now seemed more relaxed. He said, "By the way, this here's my friend Bud Shumway. Anyway, I guess I could ask you for your driver's license and maybe give you a ticket for not having plates or something, or for speeding. Maybe impound your plane." He grinned, adding, "I've always wanted to take up flying."

Cherokee laughed, though a bit strained, then said, "Listen, son, when I figure out what's going on and get it fixed, I'll take you up for a flight."

"No kidding?" Howie sounded like a little kid. "I've never been up in a plane."

"No way!" Cherokee replied, slapping Howie on the back like a long-lost buddy. "Well, we can sure fix that." He turned and smiled at Bud. "And you're welcome to come too," he said as an afterthought. He now took a small can of tobacco from his shirt pocket and a package of rolling papers and began rolling a cigarette.

Howie stopped, looking at Bud for a moment as if thinking, then took a business card from his pocket, handing it to Cherokee, who then did the same.

Bud figured they were now officially on their way to starting a mutual admiration society. He had a suspicion Howie's admiration was maybe a bit more genuine than Cherokee's.

Howie beamed, then turned to Bud. "Say, Sheriff, you mind gettin' on the radio and contacting the sheriff? Cherokee here's gonna need an escort on down the road to the airport, and it's out of my jurisdiction."

Cherokee looked at Bud, a hint of confusion in his face, then said to Howie, "I thought you were sheriff. That's what your badge says, 'Sheriff.' How can he be sheriff? And who's this sheriff you're gonna call?"

Howie grinned and answered, "Bud's the ex-sheriff, but I always forget and call him sheriff, that's all. I used to be his deputy. But neither of us has any jurisdiction here, cause this is Carbon County, and we're from Emery County."

Cherokee now had a look on his face that hinted of betrayal. He groaned and started kicking at an anthill by the side of the road.

Bud was now in the Land Cruiser, radioing the Carbon County Sheriff's Office, requesting an escort for the Cessna. He was soon back.

"They say you're going to have to hire a truck to haul your plane out. They can't provide an escort because they're short-handed right now," he reported. "It's about 20 miles and would take too long."

Cherokee groaned even louder.

Howie said, "Mr. Cherokee, I don't think you should kick at those poor ants like that. They didn't do nuthin' to you, and you're makin' them mad."

The red ants were now crawling up Cherokee's pant legs, and he'd dropped his cigarette and was dancing around, trying to swat them off. Bud walked over and handed Cherokee a canteen, and Cherokee then poured water on his legs, finally getting away from the ants. His pant legs now looked like Bud's did when he was irrigating.

Bud tried not to grin as he added, "You know, you're actually lucky they're making you hire your own truck, because those Carbon County boys are lots stricter than we are. They'd probably give you a ticket for landing here if they had to come out. I know, cause my granddaddy used to be the sheriff there."

Cherokee didn't say a word, but just got back in the plane and fired it up. Bud hoped he wouldn't try to fly it, but the Cessna turned around and passed the Land Cruiser, then slowly bumped down the dirt road towards Price, sans escort. Bud knew once it got to the edge of town, that would have to change, as he'd have to get on the highway to reach the airport, unless his fuel problem kicked back in before then.

Bud got back on the radio, giving Carbon County a heads up, then he and Howie started back down the road the way they'd come.

"He was sure a nice guy, wasn't he, Sheriff?" Howie said.

"You bet, Howie, but somehow I get the feeling he was flying around looking for something, and he sure didn't want us to know what it was," Bud replied.

"You think so?" Howie sounded surprised.

"I do," answered Bud. "And what did you think of his cigarette papers?"

"I didn't notice," Howie answered.

"GI Jay camos," Bud said. "But we need to get back down the road and see if we can find where those coordinates are. At this rate, we'll never figure it out, and who knows, those cloven-hoofed aliens are probably getting tired of waiting."

Howie grinned and headed back in the direction of the coordinates.

CHAPTER 13

"Bud?" Howie said, driving along. "I know that meteorite came down last night, not before, and I'll tell you how I know. I been thinking about it."

"Oh?" Answered Bud.

"Well," Howie continued, "It was the tracks. I looked around when we were back there by the tank, and our tracks from yesterday were all over the place."

Bud waited awhile, knowing it would take Howie a bit to get it out, kind of like when you waited at Howie's Drive-In when the service was slow.

Finally, Bud said, "Go on."

Howie replied, "Well, the meteorite was on top of our tracks. If it had been there before, we would've stepped on it and it would be ground down in a bit, plus there would be a small crater. But it was just laying right there."

"Good sleuthing, Sheriff," Bud said, trying to remind Howie of how important his position was. "You're really developing an eye for things."

"Thanks," Howie replied. "Are we close to the turnoff to those coordinates yet?"

"Almost," Bud said, noting the white pickup hadn't been following them back. Seems like whoever it was had gotten sidetracked up at the quarry, which was good. He wondered if Cherokee Smith had met up with any of the Carbon County deputies by now.

They dropped back down from the Morrison into the Navajo Sandstone, which comprised much of this section of the Swell and the Lost City. An old four-wheel drive road wound up and down the big domes, and Bud thought he could see someone way out there, someone in a tan vehicle, though he couldn't make out exactly what kind.

Howie also spotted it and stopped the Land Cruiser.

"Someone's out joy riding," Howie said.

"Appears so," Bud replied. "And for some reason, that rig looks familiar, but it can't possibly be who I think it is."

"Why not?"

"Because nobody in their right mind would take a Crown Vic out there. You wouldn't get it back home."

"What's those two things running ahead?" Howie asked.

Bud reached into his pack and got out his binoculars. He got out of the vehicle, as did Howie.

"Dogs. He's got dogs for spotters."

Howie laughed. "It's that Gary guy, isn't it? Looks like a great way to walk the dogs."

The tan car now slowly climbed a dome that Bud guessed to be several hundred feet high, with drop offs on either side of the narrow track. It was steep enough that Bud knew he would never dare try it without a four-by-four vehicle. Even then, it would take an expert driver to negotiate the grade, which Bud guessed to be at least 50 percent or more.

At one point, the car stopped at a steeper section, and Bud and Howie both held their breath, wondering if it could continue. Backing down that narrow sheer track would be totally terrifying, if not almost impossible.

The car backed down a few feet in order to get a better start, then slowly drove on upwards, its tires gripping the sandstone.

"He's a heck of a good driver, I'll give him that," Bud, somewhat in disbelief. "Even if a bit crazy."

The car now summited the big dome and carefully turned around, and they could see a man get out and stand, as if to survey the surrounding canyons.

"Man, he's King of the Hill, ain't he?" Howie commented.

"Yeah," Bud replied, "He sure makes it look easy. I hope he has a good set of brakes on that thing."

Now the man was back in the car and slowly heading down, the dogs still running ahead. Bud and Howie stood and watched in amazement.

Before long, the car reached the bottom of the big dome and stopped, letting the dogs in, then drove on out to the main road where Bud and Howie waited.

It was definitely Gary. He pulled up next to them and stopped, getting out.

"Afternoon, fellas," he said through the gaps in his teeth.

Bud and Howie had also gotten out, and Bud was now examining the car's tires.

He said, "Not a whole lot of tread left there, Gary. How in heck did you get that car up that steep grade? I let some of the air out of my tires when I'm doing stuff like that, gives more surface for traction. How much air pressure you use?"

Gary answered, "I dunno, just whatever's in there."

Howie whistled. "That's some real admirable driving there, sir."

"Thanks," Gary replied, "But it ain't nuthin' special. You just go slow and take your time, don't rush it. I bring my dogs out here about every day for exercise. I enjoy it, and so do they."

The dogs were hanging their big heads out the car window, grinning and panting.

Gary slapped the hood of his car. "This car's the ultimate. It goes anywhere, and nothing can stop it, not even lava."

He laughed as he pulled a package of cigarette papers from one shirt pocket, then a small pouch of tobacco from the other. He laid a paper out on the car hood and sprinkled tobacco onto it.

He continued, "Ford made the biggest mistake it ever made when it quit making the Crown Vic. They killed it themselves with no advertising. If they'd just upgraded it a bit, they could've owned the police car market forever."

He was now licking the paper, having rolled it into a cigarette shape. Howie was studying the process carefully.

Gary added, "I love the Crown Vic, because the engine compartment is big, the engine is big, and it's easy to work on."

He now put the completed cigarette in his mouth and struck a match on the bottom of his boot.

Bud said, "Well, I never thought I'd see the day a Crown Vic would go up a grade like that. And like Howie said, it's not all the car, either, but a good experienced driver."

Gary looked a bit embarrassed and changed the subject.

"Say, any word on anything about Wanda? I think Ray's about to go nuts over there at the cafe. See, this UFO bunch came over from Junction, and they're keeping him busy, eatin' him out of house and home, which is good, I guess, but he needs her back again to help."

"I can imagine," Bud said. "We saw all the cars when we came by earlier. Maybe he can hire you to help out."

"Oh, I ain't much of a cook," Gary replied. "Well, I need to get on home."

Howie asked, "Where's home, Gary?"

Gary answered, "I live in that old trailer out behind the old cemetery up on the hill above the cafe."

"That's your place?" Bud replied. "I wondered who lived there."

Gary said, "Yeah, I got it real cheap when I was out visiting my mom in Wisconsin a few years ago. Almost free, actually, fifty dollars. It had three big holes in the floor—was used as an ice-fishing cabin. So I had to fix those up. Hauled it back here with this same old Crown Vic. Had to weld a hitch on it first."

He patted the car's hood, then walked around to the rear, pointing at the hitch receiver.

"Anyway, gotta run. See you boys later."

With that, he got back in and spun out, driving like a mad man on down the road, the dogs' heads hanging out the side window.

Howie and Bud got back into the Land Cruiser and continued on behind him.

"Sheriff," Howie commented, "Did you see what he was doing?"

Bud replied, "Rolling a smoke?"

"Yeah, but did you notice what kind of papers?"

"Not really. Was it the same camo kind?"

"No, worse. They had a U.S. flag on them."

"Oh," Bud answered. "I've seen that kind. It's called USA Flag papers. Ernie down at the American Legion uses them."

"No kidding?" Howie squeaked. "Isn't it illegal to burn the flag, Sheriff?"

"Well, Howie, rolling papers aren't really the same thing as the flag, last I looked."

Howie relaxed. "So, roll one for freedom, huh, Sheriff?"

Bud replied, "Ernie's a pretty patriotic guy, so I doubt he'd do anything that he shouldn't in that department."

They drove along in silence for a bit, and Bud noted once again it was getting late, just like the previous day when they'd been out here. It didn't look like they were ever going to check out those coordinates.

Finally, Howie said thoughtfully, "You know, Sheriff, there's something about that Gary guy that just doesn't set right with me. He seems kind of off, you know, maybe crooked as a dog's hind leg."

"Gary?" Bud said in surprise. "Oh, I don't know, Howie. I think he's just one of those guys who travels solo, both literally and figuratively."

"How so?"

"Well, you know, he's a loner, and he also kind of makes up his own rules as he goes along. Probably harmless. Turn here, Howie, we're at that little draw."

They turned and drove up a rough two-track that led up a draw that stopped below the flanks of Cedar Mountain.

"The coordinates are right up under that cliff face there," Bud said, looking at his GPS.

They got out in the evening shadows and began the short climb up a steep slope under a small band of cliffs, all the while looking for prints and clues of anything different.

Finally, Bud stopped near an old gnarly juniper tree and just stood there for awhile, trying to acclimate his eyes to the shadows. It appeared there was someone sitting there, but he couldn't quite tell.

"Howie," Bud said quietly, his hand on the Ruger in his shoulder holster. "Come on over here."

Bud could now make things out a bit better, and there was definitely someone sitting under the tree. They were now moaning, as if in pain.

Howie was soon there, also squinting and trying to make out what was going on. Bud was now under the tree, trying to help the guy. It was not anyone Bud knew, and he appeared to be in serious trouble, though there was no obvious wound or anything.

"What's up?" Bud asked. "Are you OK?"

The man groaned again, then mumbled something Bud couldn't quite understand. Now Howie was crouched down beside him, his hand on the guy's pulse.

The man spoke again, mumbling, "My arm's numb, tingles. Face tingles. Started in my fingers, then worked up. Please, help me. And there's Therizinosaur feathers."

With that, he slumped down even more.

Howie said grimly, "Sheriff, it appears his pulse just stopped. Do you think he might be dead?"

CHAPTER 14

Bud and Howie sat in the No Delay Cafe while Ray tried to attend to a cafe packed with people. Bud had the feeling that Ray was also the cook, which would mean their dinner would be a long time coming.

Bud was still in a bit of shock, thinking about the guy under the juniper tree. He'd begun CPR while Howie had radioed for an ambulance, but it appeared that nothing they did had helped, as the EMTs pronounced the man dead when they arrived. They had then loaded him into the ambulance and taken him on back to Price.

Now Bud and Howie sat, silently studying the menu, glumly waiting for Ray to take their order. Neither had much of an appetite, but Bud knew they should eat before going home, as there probably wouldn't be much there, just salads and carrot sticks. He wondered how long it would take before Pierre and Hoppie would start to chase him, thinking he was a rabbit.

The people in the booth next to them were discussing something, and Bud couldn't help but overhear.

"Well," said a voice Bud thought he recognized from the group at the state park, "The proof that there is intelligent life in the universe is that they haven't made contact with us yet."

Someone else said, "Can't you just see the alien state department issuing travel warnings throughout the galaxy to avoid Earth at all cost?"

Now another said, "I've always wondered why aliens have such big heads and little bodies."

Now Bud recognized Lillian's voice.

"It's because their brains are so big. All the body is good for is hauling the brain around. Someday they'll just be big round heads floating around with no bodies."

Someone that sounded like Dewey asked, "What about their hands? They'd still need hands."

Lillian replied, "Not necessarily, if they can teleport and move stuff with their brains. Or maybe they'll be big heads with arms and hands and nothing more, just floating around. But where's that waiter dude? I thought this was the No Delay Cafe. Man, this place is bonkers."

Bud now noticed that Howie seemed distracted, and sure enough, Howie then asked in a quiet confidential voice, "Sheriff, do you think that guy was murdered?"

Bud thought for awhile, then answered. "I just don't know, Howie. We won't know until we get a coroner's report. But let's keep mum about it for now."

Howie shook his head in agreement, then said, "Man, I have too much on my mind—a missing person case, the regular stuff that goes on around the office, and now maybe a murder, not to mention all our band stuff. We're supposed to get together tonight, and I need some time to practice my yodeling. I usually do that when I'm driving around town on patrol, but I haven't been on patrol since this all started. I'm beginning to see why you wanted to quit and be a melon farmer."

THE NO DELAY CAFE

Bud replied, "Well, I usually didn't have this much going on."

Ray finally made it over to Bud and Howie's booth and sat down by Bud, looking frustrated and harried.

"Man, this is totally FUBARed," Ray said, wiping sweat from his brow. "It's feast or famine. We haven't had any business at all, and now the place is packed. I sure wish Wanda was here."

"Is her cousin helping you any?" Bud asked.

Ray guffawed, "Now, that's a joke. Scrapper? I didn't even know Wanda had a cousin around here, and he shows up out of the blue. He's the laziest guy I've ever met. Only time I see him around is over at the house sleeping in the spare bedroom, playing on Wanda's computer, or coming over here wanting a free meal. Don't get me wrong, he's family, and there's something about him that I find kind of likable, though I have no idea why, but when I ask him for help he says he has to go look for Wanda, he's worried sick about her. Well, guess what? I am too, but I still have a cafe to run."

"What's up with all the business?" Howie asked. "Did you run an ad or something?"

Ray answered, "No, I'm not sure what's going on. All of a sudden a bunch of people from Grand Junction started showing up, and more keep coming all the time. Some kind of UFO club or something, from the way they talk. I guess they must've heard about that blue light over the cafe the other night."

"Didn't you send them a report that Wanda's missing?" Bud asked.

Ray looked surprised. "No."

"Well," Bud continued. "Someone filed a UFO abduction report on their website. We overheard them talking about it last night at the state park. I just figured it was you."

Ray now stood up, looking disgusted. "Well, that explains it. I know Scrapper did it. Thanks a lot, Scrapper," he said.

"Don't you need the business?" Howie asked.

"Oh, sure, it's nice, but not without Wanda here to help," Ray answered sullenly. "Anyway, what'll you boys have?"

Howie replied, "I'd like a chicken-fried steak. But if Wanda were here, you wouldn't have the business, right?"

Bud said, "Too bad you don't have spaghetti and meatballs. I guess I'd like the chicken with dumplings and gravy, Ray. That sounds really tasty."

"That's a special Wanda made up," Ray replied. "She calls it the Plucked Dumpling. I hope I can make it like she does. Dang that woman, I wish she'd come on home." Ray went on back to the kitchen.

Howie asked, "What's FUBAR?"

Bud replied, "Fouled Up Beyond All Recognition. And I think we're going to have a bit of a wait for our dinner, Sheriff."

"Even at that it beats what we'd get at home," Howie replied.

Ray was soon back out with their dinners, which surprised Bud. He was now wearing an apron, which read, "She Who Must Be Obeyed." Noting Howie's questioning look, Ray said, "This is Wanda's, not mine. She's the cook here—or was, anyway."

He then added, "I need to know what you think of this," as he pulled something from his shirt pocket beneath the apron. It was a postcard, and he started to hand it to Bud, then reconsidered and gave it instead to Howie, who examined it.

"It's nice," Howie commented. "Nice photo of the Green River Geyser. I wish I could see that darn thing erupt just once."

Ray looked irritated. "No, no, not that, on the back—the message."

Howie turned it over, then said, "That's great, Ray. Wanda's OK! Good news." He then read the card to Bud:

"Dear Ray,

Don't worry. Be home soon, will explain everything. Miss you, Wanda."

Howie handed the card to Bud, who studied it for a bit. Bud then asked, "Is this her handwriting?"

"Looks like it to me," Ray answered.

"Well," Bud continued, "Given it's really from her, it's good news, but still a puzzler. Why doesn't she just come home?"

"I wish I knew the answer to that question," Ray responded with frustration, then went back into the kitchen.

"It was postmarked yesterday in Green River," Bud added. "The River Museum there is the only one that sells those kinds of cards. One of their directors makes them."

• • •

Bud and Howie were now in the Land Cruiser and on their way home in the dark. Bud pulled some Tums from his shirt pocket, thinking that maybe he'd wait until Wanda came back before he ordered Plucked Dumpling again.

"Sheriff," Howie said, the lights from the dash making his face light up all eerily. "I have a theory about that guy we found under the tree."

"Oh?" Bud replied, not really expecting an immediate answer. He decided to time it, guessing Howie would reply when they reached the railroad bridge, a mile or so on down the road.

Sure enough, Howie paused, as if thinking, then finally, just as they crossed the bridge, replied, "I think aliens killed that guy."

Bud grinned at how accurately he'd predicted the time lapse. It finally dawned on him what Howie had just said, and he again said, "Oh?"

Howie paused again, and Bud started counting the seconds...one-thousand one, one-thousand two. Maybe if he did this each time, he could get an average response time and stop getting frustrated with Howie—it would give him some parameters to work with. Bud got to one-thousand ten before Howie finally spoke.

"Well, there was no vehicle there, Bud, so they must've dropped him off there. How else would he get way out in the middle of nowhere? And there were no apparent marks on him, not that I saw, so maybe they killed him by some kind of mind control or something—or alien gases or some kind of bacteria. You know how aliens like to kill, experiment around with humans and all."

"But what motive would they have, Howie?" Bud asked.

"I don't know. Maybe he knew something, some secret they didn't want to get out. Like what he said about the feathers, whatever that meant. I've been thinking about it, and what the heck? Maybe these aliens are some kind of feathered beings called Therizinosaurs."

"I dunno, Howie, that sounds kind of like a dinosaur to me."

Bud wanted to get home and see if he could find anything about it on the internet, as he suspected it had something to do with the petrified claw in the letter.

Howie continued, "Well, and don't you find it mighty suspicious that he was right there near the coordinates when he died? Like some kind of a setup?"

Bud replied, "I've been thinking about that, and it does seem odd. But that letter came yesterday, and whoever sent it had no idea when we'd be out there looking at things, so for that guy to be there just as we showed up seems more like a coincidence to me."

"There are no coincidences, Sheriff," Howie replied solemnly, now blinking his high beams and slowing. The Land Cruiser lights now illuminated two figures standing by the highway ahead.

As they got closer, they could see that one figure was a pale blue with reflective white stripes up its sides, and its head was pure white, rounded and shiny with sharp points coming around to where its forehead and chin should be, with a sort of grill where its mouth was and a rounded bar just below its eyes. The second was identical, but a checkerboard yellow and red.

Their hands were white, hands held up telling Howie to stop.

"Aliens!" Howie gasped. "And they're commanding me to stop!"

"Howie, I think you *should* stop," Bud said.

Howie slowed and pulled the Land Cruiser over next to the pair.

"This is it, Sheriff," he moaned. "Say goodbye to Planet Earth."

CHAPTER 15

One of the beings now pulled up the faceplate of his space helmet so he could communicate with the Earthlings, looking in through Bud's open window.

"Wow, Sheriff, are we glad to see you! Thanks for stopping. We were beginning to think we'd have to start walking, and it's a long ways home."

Now the other being pulled his helmet completely off, revealing a head of dark tousled hair. He looked like a human to Bud, but Howie pushed back against his headrest, looking tense and suspicious.

The human-looking figure said, "We messed up my dirt bike on the road back there. It's totally wrecked, well, enough that we couldn't get it home. So I got on behind Joe here on his, and he just couldn't slow down like I told him, so we hit a rock and bent his front wheel. So now we're both walking. We cut across the desert to where we could see the highway lights, but nobody would pick us up here in the dark."

"You boys hop in the back," Bud replied. "I assume you're going to Green River?"

Howie now casually looked out his window, apparently looking for more Eta Aquariid meteorites, avoiding Bud's gaze. Bud was once again trying not to grin as the two dirt-bikers got into the back of the Land Cruiser.

"Yeah, you can take us to my mom's, right across from the state park. That big old two-story farm house there," said dirt-biker Joe.

"I know your mom," Bud replied. "She's on the library board with my wife, Wilma Jean. Doesn't she run the A-OK RV park—the one that used to be the KOA?"

"Yeah, that's my mom, Nancy," answered the guy. "She's going to be mad cause we're so late."

"So's my wife," Bud replied, laughing. "I'm supposed to be helping her with leagues tonight."

They were nearly to Green River when the other dirt biker asked, "So, did you guys find whoever you were looking for out there?"

"What makes you think we were looking for someone?" Bud asked, surprised.

"We saw your airplane criss-crossing all over the place. Looked like he was flying a grid, so we figured you were looking for somebody or something. Is someone lost?"

"Well, kind of," Bud replied. "But we weren't affiliated with any plane. What did it look like?"

Now Joe answered, "It was a Piper Cub. It landed right on the Green River Cutoff. We were clear up on top of Cedar Mountain—you know, where the towers are—and we could see for miles. It landed and it looked like it let somebody out, then took off again. Landed right on the road. Isn't that illegal?"

Howie now decided to join the conversation. "Not necessarily," he said. "It's OK if it's an emergency."

The other dirt biker replied, "Well, it didn't look like no emergency to me, cause he let this guy off and then took right back off."

"Can you describe exactly where it was?" Bud asked.

"Yeah, we could see pretty good. It was up this little draw that dead-ended right under the cliffs. I know that draw because I found some dino bone there once, rock-hounding with my dad."

"Dino bone?" Howie said.

Now the other dirt biker was poking Joe in the ribs, who looked irritated, then continued, "It was just scrap bone, down in the wash, but it sure looked like there might be something up above there. But we didn't have time to climb up and look, so we went home. I've been thinking about going back, but just never have."

Now Howie said, "It's illegal to find bone, you know."

Joe replied a bit testily, "Not illegal to find it, just to keep it, last I heard."

Bud interrupted, "How long ago was this?"

"Oh, I dunno, a couple of years."

They were now taking the Green River exit, and were soon by the state park, which Bud noted was almost full of campers. He suspected more UFOers had arrived.

They let the dirt bikers off at the big farm house, then Howie drove back down Kings Lane and out to Bud's bungalow. Bud noted that Wilma Jean's pink Lincoln was gone, so she must be on down at the bowling alley.

"Say, Howie," Bud said, getting out of the patrol vehicle. "I forgot, Wilma Jean's running a contest for a new name for the bowling alley. She thinks 'Green River Bowl' is boring. Have any ideas? She's giving away a free bowling ball to the winner."

Howie sat, thinking, then finally said, "How about Bowlero? Get it?" He grinned, then added, "And you could name your team 'the Bowling Stones.' Or how about the 'Spare Parts' or the 'Wrecking Balls'? Not bad for a ten-cent brain, huh?"

Bud laughed. "Not bad at all. I'll mention the Bowlero one. You think most people would get it was a play on the song?"

"Sure," Howie replied, then added, "Well, maybe not. It kinda dates me, I guess."

"Well, I'll mention it to Wilma Jean. In the meantime, let me know if you think of anything else. Speaking of which, I need to get on down there, but we still need to do some more exploring at those coordinates. You want to try again tomorrow? Seems like going out on the Cutoff is getting to be our SOP, doesn't it?"

Howie asked, "What's that?"

"Standard Operating Procedure. Give me a call."

"10-4, Sheriff," Howie replied. "And roll 'em on down the lane, er, line."

Bud turned and went through the gate and into the house, where Pierre ambushed his pant leg from behind the door, as usual, while Hoppie barked like a fool. Bud gave them each a piece of pot roast, then read the note Wilma Jean had left on the fridge door.

"Hon, dogs fed, dinner in fridge, come down at 7. XXOO"

Bud opened the fridge, noting a big glass bowl with plastic wrap over it. He took it out and examined it. Some kind of salad, he noted, glad he'd already eaten. He knew Wilma Jean would be miffed if he didn't eat it, but he wasn't at all hungry, and just looking at it made him even less so.

He stood there for a bit, not sure what to do, then took it outside to the compost pile and dumped it out, kind of kicking old compost over it so it wasn't so obvious.

Kind of ironic, he thought, a nice fresh salad going into the compost pile to help grow another one just like it, kind of a waste. He felt a bit guilty and decided that tomorrow he would get with the program and try harder to enjoy rabbit food.

He went back inside, made himself a cup of hot chocolate, and kicked back in his big easy chair. He'd take a short break, then head on down to the bowling alley. Pierre wanted up beside him, so he pulled the little weener dog up, then patted Hoppie on the head.

It had been a long day, and his intentions of getting back out to the farm had fallen by the wayside. He knew the two hired hands would make sure the irrigating got done, but he felt a bit like he was slacking on the job. And now things were getting serious out at the No Delay Cafe.

What if the guy they'd found under the juniper had been murdered? Bud knew that Howie was having trouble processing the idea that Wanda was a missing person and wasn't sure what to do with that, so how would he possibly handle something as serious as a murder?

And they still hadn't figured out what the coordinates and claw were all about. And there was the state guy in the white pickup—what was he up to? And Cherokee, the pilot who supposedly dropped someone off right where the dead man had been found—was he involved? And why did Gary and Scrapper always act so suspicious?

Bud knew there was no way he could just get back to

his quiet life and let Howie handle it all—mostly because he knew Howie wouldn't let him. Howie would be calling every half hour for advice. And yet, Howie needed to deal with this pretty much on his own to help build his confidence, and Bud really didn't want to get involved.

He sighed. This was the night for his favorite show, and he hated missing it. He got up and fiddled with the VCR, setting it up to record. He would watch Scooby Doo when he got home later.

He gave the dogs each a Barkie Biscuit, then headed out the door, thinking about the events of the day, not even aware he was again clicking the training clicker in his pocket.

CHAPTER 16

Bud stood behind the counter at the River Museum, talking to the cashier, a nice elderly woman named Irma who volunteered there as something to do to keep from getting bored.

"These are really nice cards, Irma," he said. "Do you sell a lot of them?"

Bud held a card with a photo of the Green River Geyser just like the one Ray had received from Wanda.

"Quite a few," Irma replied. "Though we don't actually sell much of anything this time of year."

Bud pulled some change from his pocket and paid for the card. He continued, "Do you know Wanda over at the No Delay Cafe, you know, the place close to the Green River Cutoff Road on the way up to Price?"

Irma paused, thinking. "No, I guess I don't. I'm not up that way much. I always go to Junction to shop."

"Well, do you recall if a short dark-haired woman came in and bought one of these recently? I know that's not much information, but she usually wears jeans and cowboy boots, has long dangly earrings."

"No, that doesn't sound familiar...but I did have a fellow come in who sounds a bit like that, except for the earrings, of course, and he was dressed in that camouflage clothing

hunters wear. Day before yesterday. I remember him because he had a stinky cigar in his mouth and I was afraid
he'd light it up in here, but he didn't."

"And he bought one of these cards?"

"Yes, he did. I remember him because he started kidding around with me. After awhile, he asked me if I was
married, and I asked him if he went to church, and that put
an end to that. He couldn't get out of here fast enough."
She smiled as if relishing how clever she'd been.

"Yeah, that's Wanda's cousin. He's a character. Name's
Scrapper."

"Well, that sure fits him," Irma added, then turned to
help another customer.

Bud was now back in his FJ, headed back to the farm,
where he'd already set the water earlier. He didn't have
much to do today, as the hired guys were weeding and
would keep an eye on the water, changing it to the next
field when it was time. Things would be slow until the
melon harvest.

He decided to stop by the bungalow. He'd had breakfast earlier over at the Chow Down, where he usually only
stopped for his mid-morning break of coffee and doughnuts. He usually ate breakfast at home, but the thought of
having hummus and crackers didn't really appeal to him,
especially since he still wasn't sure what hummus was.

He'd tried a few bites while Wilma Jean watched ap-
provingly, then told her he had to get to work, though he
instead headed for the Chow Down. What he really meant,
he told himself to stave off the guilt, was that he had to get
some decent chow so he would be able to work.

Pierre and Hoppie were there doing their usual wel-
coming committee job, barking and gnawing on his pant

leg, and Bud gave them a piece of pot roast from the fridge, then looked a bit for a snack to take out to the farm for later.

All he could find were some apples and bananas, so he stuck an apple in his shirt pocket just as his cell phone rang. He had to first remove the apple in order to get to his cell phone, which took awhile as the apple got stuck, but he finally answered.

"Yell-ow."

"Sheriff, Howie here. I didn't think you would ever answer. What're you up to today?"

"Oh, just the usual. I'm here at the house and getting ready to go back out to the farm."

"Man, I wish I could just go home and hang out like that whenever I wanted," Howie said, forgetting that there was a time when he'd wished he was sheriff so he could come and go as he pleased, back when he was Bud's deputy and holding down the fort while Bud ran around. Now that he was sheriff, he was beginning to realize that Bud hadn't been goofing off nearly as much as he'd suspected.

Bud replied, "Well, Howie, there's no law saying you can't go home once in awhile. I used to take my paperwork home and do it there."

"Oh, I know, Sheriff, but I can't. Maureen has the day off, and if I go home to work she'll put me to work."

"Well, that wouldn't be so good. You'd be working twice as hard," Bud replied, "and without overtime."

"Yeah, and I need to take some time off, not work harder. Problem is, there's nobody around to cover for me, so I can't take time off."

"Well, what can I do for you, Howie? I'm about ready to head out."

"Oh, I dunno, Sheriff. I've been thinking about everything out at the No Delay Cafe, and I can't make sense of anything. I just got the coroner's report back."

Just like Howie, Bud thought, saving the important stuff for last.

"And?" Bud asked. He started silently counting, one-thousand one, one-thousand two...

Howie answered at about one-thousand six, making Bud think things might be picking up a bit, as the last time it had gone all the way to one-thousand ten.

"Well, it says this guy died of a heart attack. His name's George Mills, and he's from Price, age 76. He was a retired heavy equipment mechanic. Worked for the mines. What should I do now, Sheriff?"

"Well, I don't know. What do you think you should do?"

"I dunno. Maybe get some more info on him, talk to his wife or somebody, but how do I go about that?"

"Howie, you can contact the sheriff up in Price and they'll help you out."

"Oh sure, I thought of that, but wasn't sure. Say, you doing anything today?" Howie asked.

"Just the usual. But Howie, why do you need more info if he died of a heart attack? Do you suspect something?"

"Bud, something's wrong. He said his arm was numb and his face tingled."

"Well, isn't that typical of a heart attack?"

"I dunno."

Bud sighed. Getting information from Howie reminded Bud of when he was back in school and had to diagram sentences—you did it slowly, tortuously, one sentence at a time.

Finally, Howie continued, "He said it started at his fingers and worked up. Sheriff, if he'd had a heart attack, wouldn't it go the other direction? I mean, since his heart stopped, wouldn't that area be numb first, then it go down the line as the circulation was cut off?"

Bud answered, "Well, I don't know. It seems to me that the stuff furthest from the heart would be the first to lose circulation. You need to talk to a doctor."

Howie was quiet for a moment, then said, "Well, I still think it had something to do with aliens. I think whatever they were doing to George, trying to kill him probably, ended up scaring him to death. All those UFO people aren't here just for nothing, they know something's going on—they stay on top of this kind of stuff. But say, Sheriff, would you mind doing me a favor?"

"Sure, Howie, go ahead."

"Would you go back out to the coordinates with me? I'm kind of afraid to go out there alone after all that's happened."

"Well, sure, Howie. You probably shouldn't go out there alone. Come on by and pick me up," Bud said.

"OK, and I need to stop by the No Delay Cafe and see if I left my cell phone out there."

"What are you calling from?" Bud asked.

"I'm on the phone at the office, and Maureen will be pretty mad at me if she finds out, as this would be the second one this month. It's that ten-cent brain, you know."

"Why don't you call out there and see if Ray found it?"

"Oh, I did, and he said he's too busy to look."

"Too busy?"

"Yeah, he said there was an accident last night at the cafe, and he's trying to clean up the mess."

"An accident?" Bud asked.

"Yeah, he thinks his sign out front was used for target practice by an alien ship. Whatever it was, it blasted it to smithereens, and it had to be large to destroy something that big."

"More aliens," Bud sighed. "Well, maybe you should bring some more sandwiches in case we get abducted."

"That's a big can do," Howie replied cheerfully. "And Sheriff, bring some more of that secret-recipe coffee in case we get lost in some distant galaxy and are up all night."

CHAPTER 17

Bud started a pot of coffee brewing, and while waiting for Howie, decided to search on the internet and see what a Therizinosaur was. It didn't take long, and it was, as he suspected, a dinosaur.

"Therizinosaurs (reaping lizards) are dinosaurs whose fossils have been found in Cretaceous deposits in Mongolia, China, and Western North America. Various features of the forelimbs, skull, and pelvis unite fossil specimens as theropods and maniraptorans, close relatives to birds.

Among the most striking characteristics of Therizinosaurs are the large claws on their hands, which reached lengths of three feet. The unusual range of motion in Therizinosaur forelimbs, which allowed them to reach forward to a degree other theropods could not achieve, also supports the idea that they were mainly herbivorous. Therizinosaurs may have used their long reach and strongly curved claws to grasp and shear leafy branches. There is however, to date, no evidence of the Therizinosaur having feathers."

Bud unconsciously began clicking the training clicker in his pocket, thinking. No feathers, and yet the man under the juniper tree had distinctly said, "Therizinosaur feathers."

Was it possible he'd found something that would link the Therizinosaur more strongly to birds? Had he found evidence of feathers? Why else would he say that, Bud wondered.

He then did a search on maniraptorans.

"Maniraptora (hand snatchers) is a group of dinosaurs that first appear in the fossil record during the Jurassic and are regarded as surviving today and are represented by about 10,000 species of living birds."

Just then, Bud heard Howie drive up. He shut down the computer and quickly poured the coffee into the thermos, added some vanilla ice cream, and headed out the door, his Ruger in its shoulder holster under his jacket.

He paused, as Hoppie and Pierre were now barking and whining, feeling sorry for themselves for being left behind.

Bud walked over to the Land Cruiser and said, "Hey, Howie, let's take my rig this time. The dogs really need to get out, if you don't mind me taking them along."

Howie replied, "No, Sheriff, I sure don't mind one bit. That way whoever was following us will maybe be thrown off by the different vehicle with more occupants. Gotta keep 'em guessing, I guess."

Bud opened the porch door and Hoppie and Pierre tumbled out, excited to be going. Bud went back inside and grabbed some dog biscuits and a water jug, then came back out and helped little Pierre into the back seat of the FJ, next to Hoppie.

He stopped at the East Winds and gassed up, then they were soon on the freeway, taking the exit for Price.

Bud said, "Howie, we had my FJ the first time we were followed, so we're not very incognito, but let's not stop by the cafe until we come back, and maybe we can go out there unnoticed for once."

Howie nodded in agreement, then started humming and tapping his fingers on the dash.

"We had a real good practice session last night, Sheriff," he said. "My new songs are sounding pretty good, if I don't mind saying so. You need to come be our drummer. Maybe if things don't work out for me as sheriff I can make some money as a songwriter."

Bud replied, "Howie, why wouldn't things work out as sheriff?"

Howie thought for a moment, then said, "Well, you know, if I can't solve this case, then maybe it's a sign that I really shouldn't be in law enforcement."

"You mean Wanda? The missing person case?" Bud asked.

"No, well, yes, that, too, but I'm thinking more of this murder we have on our hands."

They were now crossing the railroad bridge, and Bud could see a big long train in the distance, but this time it was coming towards them. He pulled over on the edge of the road and got out his Canon camera. He then stopped, as if registering what Howie had just said.

"Murder? You think that guy was murdered?"

"I do, Sheriff, I really do. I called up to Price this morning and ordered some toxicology tests."

"You think he was poisoned?"

"Well, why else would he complain like that? I talked to the doc down at the clinic in Green River, and he said the tingling was a heart attack symptom, and he said it could start at the fingers and go up, but something's wrong, Bud. I need to figure it out."

Bud whistled a slow drawn-out whistle, just as the train came by and whistled back. He hung out the window, taking photos as it passed by.

Finally, he replied, "Well, I don't know about that, but you have to trust your gut in these things. I guess you'll know when you get the tests back."

"Yeah, but in the meantime, I have to proceed as if it's murder. I don't want to give the murderer any time to foul things up."

"Foul things up?"

"You know, destroy evidence and all that. And I bet it has something to do with that guy in the white pickup, and probably Scrapper and Gary, if my hunch is right. And probably that Cherokee guy, too. They're all connected somehow. And they have something to do with the aliens, is my bet. I know you don't believe in them, but I have to consider every angle. Like you used to say, a sheriff has to be thorough."

"It's a puzzle, that's for sure," Bud replied. "But say, I'm gonna turn here at this little dirt road coming up in about a quarter mile. It connects with the Cutoff Road and we'll avoid going by the cafe that way and be less likely to be seen."

Bud turned off on an indistinct old dirt road that paralleled the railroad tracks. It curved around and went behind a small hill that hid them from the cafe, then connected with the Cutoff Road.

They hadn't gone down it more than a half mile when Bud noticed someone behind them. He couldn't make out much through the dust, but it appeared that someone had also taken the road not long after they did. This gave Bud pause, as the road was basically abandoned, and only a few locals even knew it existed.

Before long, they were on the Cutoff Road, and the dust lessened, as the dirt was more packed.

"Howie, take a look behind and see if you can make out who's following us," Bud said.

After a moment Howie answered, "It appears to be someone in a red Jeep, Sheriff. Kind of looks like an old CJ, red body, black top. My uncle used to have one. You suppose they're following us?"

"Seems like it," Bud said.

"We're sure popular, huh?" Howie grinned.

"Yeah," Bud replied, "And I'm thinking it all has to do with those coordinates and that claw. Somebody knows we know something, and they want to know it, too. Problem is, we actually don't have a clue. Let's ditch them, Howie."

Bud hit the brakes and quickly turned off the road, barely slowing, the FJ careening. He drove up a wash, tires spinning a bit in the sand, then pulled up behind a big rock. The road had curved just enough when he drove off it that the Jeep didn't see them and was soon on past, continuing up the road.

They sat there for a bit, letting the dust settle.

"I'm not really sure they were following us, but if they were, that'll put an end to that," Bud said, getting out and opening the back door and letting the dogs out.

"Let's take a little break and do some rock hounding, make sure we've lost them," Bud said, starting up the wash, the dogs excitedly sniffing around and checking everything out.

They slowly walked on up the wash, and Bud suddenly had that old feeling he used to get when out wandering around the country, that feeling of pure freedom and no stress.

It was a beautiful day, and big white fluffy clouds punctuated the bluebird sky like puffs of cotton candy. Bud was in his element, and the dogs loved it, too. They were all excited, running around and sniffing things.

"Get the stick," Bud encouraged Pierre, who was tugging on the bottom branch of a blackbrush, trying to break it off, even though the branch was twice his size. Hoppie was eyeing some ravens who floated overhead, checking them out.

"Get the birds, Hoppie, get those doity boids, "Bud said to the little dog.

Howie also appeared to be enjoying himself, and as if to verify this, he said, "Say, I've been feeling kind of creative, and I thought of another name for the bowling alley."

"Oh?" Bud asked.

"The Fruit Bowl."

Bud didn't say anything, as he wasn't sure what to say.

Howie continued, "Or how's about Ten Pin Alley? Or Nuts and Bowltz? Nuts and Pins? Arm Twisters Alley?"

Bud just groaned.

Howie looked disappointed. "Well, I guess it's all just out of my league."

They walked for some time, examining rocks and plants and even finding a few pieces of what looked to be flint with edges that had been worked by the Native Americans long ago.

Finally, they stopped and sat on a big white sandstone rock that had tumbled from the cliffs above. They had angled around until they were under the same line of bluffs where they'd tried to find the coordinates, but were now maybe a half-mile or so further east.

Pierre lay down at Bud's feet in the shade, tired. Bud wondered how many dachshund miles were equivalent to a human mile, and he guessed that for every mile he walked, Pierre went the equivalent of about five.

Bud then noticed Hoppie was missing. He must've got sidetracked by something interesting. Bud whistled, but no Hoppie.

He waited a bit, then started up the wash, looking. But just then, the little dog came running with something in his mouth, dropping it at Bud's feet.

Bud picked it up and examined it, then said, "Howie, look here. Hoppie brought us a nice little bone—dino bone. Gem quality, too."

Bud handed Howie the piece of bone, and Howie examined it. It was a beautiful deep red color that stood out from most bones Bud had seen, which were typically gray.

"Sheriff," Howie said. "Look at this really close. It looks like the petrified dino skin I saw over at the museum in Junction, but it's different. I'm not sure what it is."

Bud took the bone back and looked more closely.

"Howie, it's different alright. It has something on it— something that looks to me to be tiny pin feathers."

CHAPTER 18

"Howie," Bud was explaining, "Most dino bone I've seen looks like bone. You can even see the cellular structure in the better samples. But this piece is all dimpled, and it really does look like tiny little feathers or down on some kind of skin. I think Hoppie may be on to something. Let's keep walking and see where it came from."

They continued on up the wash, which looked like it would soon end under the cliff face. It rapidly became choked with boulders that had fallen from the cliff, which they had to carefully negotiate.

Bud was now carrying Pierre, whose short little legs were pretty much useless with all the big rocks. Hoppie was doing better, even though his legs weren't much longer, but his bigger body gave him a bit more leverage.

They were soon forced to stop where the wash tumbled straight off the cliffs. Bud could now see a layer of impermeable sandstone some fifty feet above them, and it looked like there were a number of holes at the contact between that and the lower softer layer.

"Howie," Bud nodded towards the holes, "We need to get up there. I betcha anything that's where this bone came from."

"How can we climb up that?" Howie asked.

"I don't think we can, but I'm wondering if we couldn't maybe circle around and get above that layer somehow and come down from on top."

"There's no road up there, Bud, there can't be."

"No, I know that, but I think if we backtrack we'll be able to see a route up there."

"Is it really worth all that trouble just to see where this bone came from?" Howie asked dubiously.

"Well, think about what's on this bone, and yeah, it just might be. If we can find where this came from, we might be on to something—something that I have a hunch a few others would like to be in on."

"You mean like the guy in the white pickup?"

"Maybe," Bud answered.

"Don't you think it might be getting a bit dangerous, Sheriff?" Howie seemed more tentative. "Maybe we should get the Carbon County sheriff in on this."

"Well," Bud said, now walking back down the wash, "We're still in Emery County, so they might not be very interested. Besides, they might still be busy escorting Mr. Cherokee Smith down the road, and so far, this isn't sheriff business at all, it's more in the paleontological arena."

"You suppose we might find a new kind of dinosaur? Would they name it after us, Bud? The Howiebudsaurus? Or maybe the Budhowiesaurus?"

Bud laughed. "Well, it would be easy for us to remember the name if they did. Actually, Howie, it is a tradition to name a new species of dinosaur after whoever discovered it."

They continued down the wash and were soon back away from the cliff where they could see better. Bud stood and studied the cliffs for a bit, then said, "Howie, if we drove down the road a bit, it looks like we could backtrack and get up without much problem. Let's try it."

They were soon back at the FJ, driving on down the road, keeping a lookout for the red Jeep and white pickup, but it appeared they'd lost everyone.

Bud drove about a mile, then followed a faint track back that gradually wound up above the cliff band. He parked behind a group of junipers, trying to hide the FJ, and they got out and started hiking towards the head of the wash.

"We're really not very far from the coordinates," Bud pointed out. "The old tank is just right down there."

They continued working their way just above the cliff band until they could see the wash directly below them, the dogs at their heels. Bud picked up Pierre and handed him to Howie, saying, "Hang on to this little guy, if you don't mind, and I'll see if I can find a break in the cliffs."

Howie replied, "Why not just follow that trail?" He pointed to what looked like a somewhat indistinct animal trail that wound down through the rocks and appeared to end just below.

Bud was a bit surprised. Why would there be an animal trail here? Usually animal trails connected places animals went, and few animals would be wandering around these steep cliffs. Maybe it was a bighorn trail.

Bud said, "You know, Howie, I'm going to put the dogs back in the FJ. I have a feeling we need to look around a bit, and I want to be able to not worry about them. These cliffs are pretty heady." He took the dogs back to the FJ, leaving the windows partway down for them.

Howie had gone ahead and was already down below the cliffs by the time Bud caught back up with him.

"Sheriff, look at this. These holes look like they were dug by hand." Howie stood peering into a hole that was big enough for someone to walk into if they stooped. "We need a flashlight."

Bud walked back up to the FJ and grabbed his daypack. He was soon beside Howie again, taking a big police flashlight out of the pack.

"Someone's been digging for sure," Bud said. "It looks like someone threw dirt out of the hole and then kind of kicked it around as if trying to hide the fact that they'd been digging." Bud had carefully looked for tracks on his way down there, but had found only Howie's—but he had found what looked like broom marks, as if someone had swept away their tracks.

He now pointed the light into the hole, where he could see shovel marks. The hole appeared to go back in a good 20 feet.

"Look, Sheriff, here's what they were digging for." Howie handed Bud a rock.

"Petrified wood," Bud replied.

"It's all over the place, around the hole. They were digging for wood. That's not illegal, is it, Sheriff?" Howie asked.

"No," Bud replied. "But it's also not something anyone would dig for. Howie, you can find big petrified logs just laying around out in this country. Old Reo's got them all around his gas station down in Hanksville. Wood's not valuable enough to put this kind of effort into. Something else is going on here."

Now Bud stooped and began working his way back into the hole, even though he didn't like dark closed-in places. He hadn't gone back in more than 10 feet when he found what he suspected. He was quickly back out.

"Howie, whoever's digging here knows what they're doing is illegal. They planted the wood as a diversion, is my guess. That hole has dinosaur bones in it, and it looks like there's a lot of them."

Bud then examined the other holes.

"These are all bone digs," he confirmed. "Somebody's digging in a big way, and it looks to me like they're having a lot of luck. And look, they have camouflage nets over these two holes, which have tools in them."

"Sheriff, we need to get out of here now," Howie said in a panicky voice. He pointed to the sky, where Bud could now see an airplane in the distance, too far away to be heard, but flying low.

"I need to do one more thing," Bud replied, taking his GPS from his pack. He held it out for a moment, then said, "It says we're at 39°11'41"N and 110°34'32"W, Howie. I'm no genius with numbers, but I've studied those coordinates enough to have them memorized, and this is real close to what you got in that letter, which was 39°11'14"N and 110°34'32"W."

Bud paused, studying the plane, which was rapidly getting closer. He continued, "Whoever wrote that note made a mistake and transposed two digits—the 14 should've been a 41. I doubt very much if it was intentional. That puts us a bit more north of where we were looking, and this is where the paydirt is."

Bud paused to look at the sky. The plane was rapidly getting closer, as if it had spotted the FJ.

He said, "Let's git. We sure don't want anyone else to find this, except a paleontologist."

"Yeah, and we don't want Scrapper coming back for this," Howie said, showing Bud a cigar he'd just picked up.

CHAPTER 19

Bud and Howie had run to the FJ and quickly driven back down to the main road, pulling onto it just as the airplane flew overhead, only a few hundred feet over them. They could tell it wasn't Cherokee's Cessna, which was probably still in the shop being repaired, but Bud figured it could still be Cherokee, maybe in a different plane.

"I have a little idea, Howie," Bud said, watching the plane bank and turn as if to come back around over them. "Let's give this guy something to think about."

"I bet he's looking for that dino dig," Howie replied. "Hopefully he didn't see exactly where we were."

Bud said, "I think you may be right, but mum's the word. We can't mention what we found to anyone, not even our wives. Not until we figure out what's going on. Then we'll get the state paleontologist down here. I have a feeling this is a major find."

"Sheriff," Howie said, "Do you suppose that guy who was murdered is the same one who sent the letter with the coordinates?"

"I don't know," Bud replied. "It was postmarked Radium, but someone could've mailed it from there to throw us off, to not incriminate themselves. George Mills lived in

Price. I think we should go on up there and visit his wife, but first let's see if we can help that plane find what he's looking for."

Bud drove up the road a few miles, then pulled over next to the ruins of an old cabin that set up against the cliffs. There wasn't much left of it, as the roof had collapsed, and cattle had used the remaining posts to scratch against, pushing them over.

He parked the FJ and let the dogs out, then opened the back and pulled out a shovel. The plane had now circled around and was again flying over them. Bud walked over to the edge of a small depression and began to dig.

"What's in there?" Howie asked, puzzled.

Bud replied, "This old cabin belonged to a friend of my grandpa, an old uranium miner. The cattle just basically destroyed it, using it for their lounge. Anyway, my grandpa told me that this old guy, his name was Cactus Ed, he had a big can dump about right here where I'm digging."

"A can dump?" Howie asked.

"Yeah, you know, a place where he threw his cans. These old guys lived mostly on canned goods, going into town and stocking up only every few months. Can dumps are a Western institution in this country. This one has kind of silted under through the years, though. You go out by some of these old uranium mines and you'll see the can dumps right where they threw the cans out the window of the mine shack. Pretty handy, I guess. Their motto was 'Just fling it.'"

Bud had now dug a few feet into the ground, and he pulled out an old rusted can with corrugated sides, its label long gone. As he dug, the airplane cruised directly overhead. He looked up and pretended to try to hide his shovel, leaning it against the FJ and acting nonchalant.

"So, Sheriff," Howie asked, "Is this what you'd call a ruse?"

"Sure is, Howie," Bud answered. "If we can get that plane to decide this is what we're out here for, maybe they'll quit following us around. But we don't really need to go searching out here anymore anyway, cause we now know what we were looking for."

"The dino dig?"

"Yup," Bud replied. He was now digging again, and he pulled out what looked to be another old can. It was round and squat and had a faded label with the words 'Grizzly Chew.'

"This one's ABC," he said, throwing it back into the hole.

"What's that?" Howie asked.

"Already Been Chewed. But say, what say let's get on up to Price and see what we can find out from George's wife? Maybe we can have lunch up there while we're at it. There's a really good place out in Wellington called the Cowboy Kitchen that me and Wilma Jean like when we go up that way."

Howie grinned, and Bud got the dogs into the FJ and they headed on up the road, noting that the plane was now circling where they'd just been, as if trying to get a fix on the location.

It didn't take long to get to Price, and Howie called the sheriff there and got George's wife's number, then called her and asked if they could come and talk for a bit.

She lived in a small house on the outskirts of town, in a picturesque area called Spring Glen, and it wasn't long before Bud and Howie were sitting in her front drive.

The house was older but well kept, surrounded by several acres of hayfields. The front lawn was bordered by flower beds that were just starting to bloom in shades of purples and reds.

They got out of the FJ as a small slim woman came out of the front door, dressed in white fluffy slippers and a flowery yellow muumuu-type dress printed with giant red orchids.

She held out her hand and introduced herself. "Afternoon. I'm George's wife, Betty. I'm not sure what I can do for you, but you fellas are welcome to come on in."

Howie said, "That's OK, Mrs. Mills. We don't want to take up much of your time, maybe just ask a few questions, if that's OK."

"Well, of course, but call me Betty."

She motioned for them to sit down in some lawn chairs on a flagstone patio by the front garden.

She then said, "Don't mind the way I'm dressed. I just don't want to get myself made up anymore, now that George's gone. I just want to stay home all the time."

She looked to Bud like she was going to start crying any minute.

Bud said, "Well, that's certainly understandable, seeing what you're going through. We won't keep you long. Can you tell us a bit about George's heart? Was it in pretty bad shape?"

Betty looked puzzled. "His heart? No, he had a good heart. In fact, the doctor had just done tests on him for his annual physical, which was actually more like his every ten-year physical, as much as he hated going to the doctor. But they gave him a clean bill of health."

Bud replied, "You mean he had a good heart? You do know the coroner said he died of a heart attack, don't you?"

"Yes, they told me that," she answered. "I called his doctor and they said it's not unheard of for a person to die that way even with a good heart once you get to be our age. Are you fellas thinking something else was going on?" She now looked concerned.

Howie replied, "Maybe, but we don't know. It just seemed odd that he would die like that—to me, anyway."

Now Betty looked even more concerned. "Die like what?"

Howie continued, "Well, we were there with him for the last few minutes, and he said something about a dinosaur and it just seemed odd."

Now Betty smiled fondly, as if remembering her husband. "That George, he was a total nutcase for rockhounding and finding dinosaur bone and gizzard stones and things like that. He had a lapidary outfit set up in the spare bedroom and liked to polish stones and make bolo ties and such. That's what he did in the evenings and in the winter. When the weather was good, he spent all of his time out running around, when he wasn't gardening, anyway. He was sure a guy for hobbies. Nothing wrong with his mind."

Bud asked, "Did he have a buddy he went out with?"

Betty replied, "Oh sure, he had several. They all belonged to the local rock club. They were all alike, rocks for brains, nothing made them happier than looking for rocks. I'd always ask George where they were going each time, how far, and he'd just say, 'a smile and a half hither, thither, and yon.' He was a cheerful guy and everybody liked him. I sure miss him."

"Did he know a guy named Cherokee Smith?" Bud asked.

"Not that I recollect," Betty answered. "But that doesn't mean much. A bunch of them would get together every Saturday and go out, and I have no idea who they all were. A lot of them were fellow Masons, and I never did understand that deal, not one bit. Kind of a secretive bunch. I didn't mind his rock club, but that Mason stuff was a bit far out for me, and he knew it. My best friend Marla feels the same exact way. All those secret rituals and grown men wearing silly hats and robes and chanting..."

Bud could see they weren't going to get much farther on the information front, so he leaned back in his chair and surveyed the gardens that wound around the big lawn. Finally, he said, "You know, George must have been quite the gardener. These flower beds are really beautiful. Or do you garden also?"

Betty answered, "Oh, I garden a lot, but my garden is out back—I do vegetables. The flowers are all George's. He loved flowers to his dying day. In fact, he had just gone up to Bruin Point the day he died to transplant some wildflowers into the garden, the ones you see over in that corner."

She pointed to a flowerbed filled with long-stemmed purple flowers planted between a ceramic frog and a giant red plastic ladybug on a stick.

They all sat in silence for a bit until Howie stood.

"Well, Mrs. Mills," he said, gently taking her hand, "Thank you for having us over and answering our questions. If we find out anything unusual, you'll be the first to know."

Now Betty again looked like she was going to cry. She took Howie by both hands and just stood there for a moment, gathering herself, then said, "You know, the reason George was so darn healthy was because he ate so well. We had a big salad for dinner every night, fresh from my garden. You boys stay right here, and I'm gonna go get you each a sack of fresh-picked vegetables for your dinner."

With that, she turned and went into the house. They soon heard the back screen door slam. Betty was soon back with a big grocery sack for each, filled to the brim with the same kind of stuff that Bud had buried in the compost pile. They took the sacks, thanking her, as she showed them out.

Bud was beginning to feel a bit persecuted, but he knew that could easily be fixed with a stop at the Cowboy Kitchen for one of their prime rib-eye steaks.

They thanked Betty and were soon on their way.

CHAPTER 20

Bud sat at the kitchen table, trying his best to drink the smoothie Wilma Jean had just made for him. He had sipped it a bit and was now fiddling with the clicker in his pocket.

Wilma Jean came back into the kitchen and looked at his almost full glass, then said, "Hon, it's really tasty. You just have to give it a chance."

Bud replied, "But it's green."

Wilma Jean laughed. "Green is good. It's full of antioxidants and stuff that'll make you healthy."

"What's in it?" Bud asked, though he really didn't want to know. He took another sip, trying not to gag. It was like drinking liquid alfalfa. He was glad he and Howie had managed yet another good solid dinner last night at the Cowboy Kitchen, and at least he wasn't starving to death yet.

"I made it from all that stuff you brought home yesterday. Spinach, broccoli, and kale, and I threw in an apple to sweeten it up. I'll use watermelon when they get ripe."

"Oh, good, good," Bud replied, "You on your way down to the cafe? I'm going to finish this yummy stuff all up, then get out to the farm." He lifted the glass and pretended to drink.

She squeezed his shoulder and headed out the door, much to Bud's relief, and he went over to the kitchen sink, starting to pour the smoothie out. Just then, she came back in. He quickly held the glass back up to his mouth as if still drinking, then said, "Almost done here, just gonna rinse out the glass and get going."

Wilma Jean stopped and looked at him. "Bud Shumway, you better not pour that out after all the trouble I went to making it."

"No, no, I would never pour something this good out, Hon, you know that."

Bud was thinking he needed to become less predictable. Wilma Jean knew him too well.

She stood silently watching him until he finished the smoothie, then she left again. Bud rinsed out the glass, feeling kind of half sick. He wondered how something so good for you could taste so bad.

Just then, his phone rang.

Bud thought later, in his own defense, that he'd been in a bit of shock from trying to get the smoothie down and wasn't thinking clearly, or he would've immediately tried to get more information from the caller.

"Yell-ow," Bud answered.

"Is this Bud Shumway?"

It was a woman's voice, one that sounded vaguely familiar.

"It is," Bud answered. "What can I do for you?"

"Bud, this is Wanda from the No Delay Cafe. You remember me, don't you?"

Bud was speechless. He finally managed to stammer, "Of...of course!"

"Well, I don't know what to do. I'm calling you because you used to be sheriff, and I thought maybe you could give me some advice. Your deputy just doesn't inspire confidence, or I'd call him instead."

"I'll help if I can, Wanda. What's the problem?" Bud asked.

"Things are getting totally out of control. This wasn't at all how I planned it to be, and now I don't know how to deal with it. It's getting dangerous. I'm being followed."

"Wanda, where are you? Are you aware that Ray is beside himself worrying about you?"

"Oh, I know it as well as anyone, and I do feel bad about it, but he's just got to learn how to handle things himself. Time to grow up and deal with life, no leaning on little Wanda to do everything. But there's some guy following me all over, and I know he's dangerous. What should I do?"

"Wanda, I can't help you until you tell me more about where you are. I have no idea what's going on."

"If I tell you, will you prom..."

Just then the phone went dead. Wanda had hung up.

Bud stood there staring blankly at his phone for a bit, just like in the movies, until he recovered himself. He then went into the living room and set down in his big easy chair, kicking out the footrest, trying to think.

This was totally out of the blue. Why did Wanda call him and ask for help, and then hang up before he could even tell her what to do? Had someone discovered her talking on the phone and made her hang up? Or had she seen someone coming and hung up before they could see her?

Had she been kidnapped? If so, why would someone be following her? And why was she so unconcerned about

Ray's feelings? It was a puzzle, and one he didn't have enough information to solve.

He sat there for awhile, Pierre wanting up into his lap and Hoppie sleeping under the footrest. Bud felt like he needed to do something, not just sit, as it was too early in the day to kick back, but he felt kind of bloated from the smoothie.

He reached into his shirt pocket and pulled out a couple of Tums, then leaned back again, his head leaning against the soft red and green striped afghan draped across the back of the chair, one of Wilma Jean's earlier attempts. The stripes were a bit crooked, but it was comfortable just the same.

He wondered why Howie hadn't called him yet, as it was beginning to be a daily thing. Maybe he didn't have anything new to report. They had stopped by the No Delay Cafe on their way home the previous evening, where sure enough, Howie had left his cell phone, which had several messages from Maureen wanting to know where he was.

They had also asked Ray about his cafe sign, which had reportedly been used for target practice by aliens, but come to find out, had instead been hit by a big semi that swerved to miss a car turning into the cafe's parking lot.

The sign had indeed been reduced to smithereens, but apparently there had been no real harm done to the truck, as it had caught the sign with its heavy bumper.

Bud picked up the TV remote and clicked it on. He decided to watch the episode of Scooby Doo he'd recorded the other night, then get on out to the farm. He needed some time for the smoothie to settle.

For some reason, the way he felt reminded him of the time he'd been working up on the Nutter Ranch when he was on summer vacation from high school, helping his grandpa, who was the ranch manager, and the milk cow had gotten into the alfalfa field.

She'd bloated up so bad they'd had to call the vet, who came out and inserted a stomach tube. It was just in the nick of time, as her life was in danger, the vet had told them.

Bud wondered if Wilma Jean would feel bad if she came home to find the doctor there, treating Bud with a stomach tube for the effects of drinking her alfalfa smoothie.

Bud was now clicking the clicker in his pocket, and it dawned on him that he had yet to even begin to try training the dogs with it. He leaned forward, clicking it while telling Pierre to get the rabbits, but the little dog just opened one eye as if to see if Bud were serious or not, then went back to sleep.

Bud now realized he wasn't paying attention to the TV at all, and he shut it off, even though it was his favorite show. His mind wouldn't stop working—he had a hunch he needed to check out, and it was a hunch that would involve a trip out to the No Delay Cafe.

CHAPTER 21

Bud knew that if one went around the back of the old gas station building housing the No Delay Cafe and looked around, they would see a couple of old tumbled down houses, some rusted out vehicles, and a house trailer with sagging front steps, which is where Ray and Wanda (and now Scrapper) lived. In back was a fenced pasture that held Buck, who spent most of his time lazily sleeping under an old locust tree.

Bud had spent a few afternoons kicking around behind the cafe, an area that had once been a small town called Creekside, called that for its position near the banks of the Price River, a small waterway that came down from the mountains above Price.

After doing a bit of research down at the Green River library, Bud had discovered that Creekside had once flourished and was home to about 200 people who farmed the nearby desert, using a small irrigation system that utilized water from the river.

The town's main business was the railroad, which had built a depot and hotel there in the late 1800s, providing an overnight stop for travelers. The buildings were long gone, but Bud had found an old brick with "D&RGRR"

stamped onto it, one of the last remnants of the Denver & Rio Grande.

The town had repeatedly flooded, which eventually led to its demise, as people finally gave up and left for the more prosperous towns of Price and Green River. About all that now remained of Creekside was the old gas station, which had eventually been converted into the No Delay Cafe—that, and an old cemetery on top of a small nearby hill.

It was up the road to this cemetery that Bud was now driving his FJ, after negotiating a narrow wire gate that once held an old wire fence together. The fence had been built long ago to keep range cattle from going onto the cemetery grounds.

As Bud reached the top of the short but steep hill, he could see an old aluminum trailer sitting in a small field next to the now unkempt and abandoned cemetery. An old tan Crown Vic sat by the trailer's front door.

Bud parked and got out. But before he could knock on the door, Gary opened it and greeted him, stepping outside, his two dogs at his side, tails wagging.

"Howdy, Bud. What brings you up my way?"

The man was neither overly friendly nor cold, just matter of fact. His two German Shepherd mixes were soon sniffing around, obviously smelling Bud's dogs and, like Gary, neither friendly nor hostile, just matter of fact.

"Say, Gary," Bud replied, "I'd like to talk to Scrapper. I stopped by the cafe and Ray said he thought he was up here at your place."

"Oh, sure, he's inside. We're just hanging around drinking coffee. Come on in."

Bud followed Gary and the dogs into the trailer. Scrapper sat on an old couch with his feet up on what looked like an apple crate. A cigar was stuffed into his camo shirt pocket.

"Don't mind me if I don't get up, Bud," he said in his gravelly voice. "That darn horse stepped on my foot this morning."

"No, that's OK, Scrapper," Bud replied. "You just stay put. I won't be long, just wanted to ask you a few questions about Wanda and all. We need to get busy and find her. The sheriff's been a bit overwhelmed, but I think he's about ready to gear up on it now."

"Care for some coffee and canned cow?" Gary brought Bud a cup of coffee and handed him an open can of canned milk.

Gary then continued, "We really kind of agree, Scrapper and me and even Ray, that looking for Wanda's kind of something that should be low on your priority list, Bud. We all pretty much think she's safe with friends."

Bud poured some milk into his coffee, then looked around the trailer. It was old, but had lots of big windows and light and seemed homey enough. The walls were aluminum, but the counters and kitchen sink were a bright yellow, adding a bit of cheer to the place.

"This is a nice place you have here, Gary. What is this, an Airstream?"

Gary replied, "Nope, everybody thinks that, but it's a Silver Streak. Built better than any Airstream—well, except for the holes in the floor, that is."

He pointed to three round places in the floor that had been filled in with what looked like plywood lids, complete with rope handles. "Too bad we don't have ice fishin' around here."

Now Scrapper added, "He takes those boards out in the winter and grows his own veggies, right here in the house, like a greenhouse. Has big barrels he cut in half so they'd fit under the house, full of dirt. Pretty ingenious. Indoor gardens, complete with worms and bugs and everything."

Gary looked pleased. "Yup, and I have a nice big garden out back in the summer. Wanna see it?" He motioned to Bud to come look out the kitchen window.

Bud whistled. "That's huge. How do you water it?"

"I have a big hose going down to the river with a small gas pump down there. I call down to the cafe and Ray starts it up for me. It pumps water all the way up the hill into a big cistern. Use it for bathing and irrigating, but mostly irrigating."

Scrapper added, "Most people call that gray water, but with Gary, it's more like green water. He eats so darn many veggies he's turning green."

Bud thought of the smoothie he'd had not all that long ago. At least he was no longer in danger of having to find a doctor, but he now began to wonder what was on the menu for dinner tonight. He'd never dreaded going home for dinner before this, and he didn't like the feeling.

Scrapper continued. "Gary here, he's a hermit, or so he says, anyway, but he really spends all his time down at the cafe talking to Ray and the customers. Oh, and Wanda, too, when she's there. So how come you don't ever help Ray and Wanda out any, huh, Gary? They feed you all the time, and you never help with nuthin'."

Scrapper now put the unlit cigar in his mouth, looking pleased, like he'd finally got up the courage to call Gary on it. Bud found it a bit ironic, given what Ray had said about Scrapper not helping.

Gary replied testily, "I do help out—sometimes, anyway. Ray don't like my style, he says I'm too sloppy. And you...I mean Wanda, she's the kind who wants to do everything herself to make sure it gets done right. And I ain't no hermit, not really. But I will say that when I'm feeling down, I can always make myself happy again by thinking of all the people that are living on Planet Earth and how none of them are bothering me. Weren't bothering me, anyway."

He looked meaningfully at Scrapper and then pulled out his tobacco can and cigarette papers and started rolling a smoke.

Bud figured things were going downhill and it was about time to go, and he needed to finish with his questions.

He asked, "So, how come you boys seem to think Wanda's OK? Has she communicated with you at any time?"

Scrapper answered, "No, but Ray got a postcard from her saying she was fine. Like I told you earlier, I think she's just miffed at him and trying to make a point. She told me he didn't appreciate her. She'll come back when she feels like it."

"But you're just speculating. What if she's really in some kind of danger?" Bud asked, watching Scrapper closely.

Scrapper answered, "She's fine. I know my cousin better than anyone on Earth, and I know she's OK." He ran his fingers through his longish dark hair, which fell for a moment behind his ears, then continued. "And you know, that

Ray, he doesn't treat Wanda right. He takes her for granted. Maybe he'll appreciate her a bit more when she comes back."

Bud paused, looking hard at Scrapper's now revealed earlobes. He then replied, "Well, I'm glad to hear you think she's OK, and I hope you're right, but what would you say if I told you I just got a call from Wanda telling me she's not alright?"

Bud then stood, not waiting for their answer. "I'll show myself to the door, and thanks for the coffee. But if either of you hear from Wanda, tell her that anytime she wants to open up about what's going on, I'll be glad to help her, and I know the sheriff feels the same way. We're all worried about her."

Gary now stood and followed him outside. "Say, Bud..." He stood on the steps, as if wanting to say something and changing his mind, then said, "Want some veggies to take home for dinner?"

"No, I think I'll pass on that one, but I do appreciate it. My wife's got enough ammo already," Bud replied.

"Well, don't take what I said in there personally about wanting to be left alone, it was meant for Scrapper. We're just having our differences, and it's getting old, much as I like the guy."

Gary then held up his hand as if to wave goodbye, but just stood there, hand up, as if frozen in time.

Bud replied, "It's OK. And I'm pretty sure I know where Wanda is now."

With that, Bud got into his FJ and drove on back down the hill. He could see Gary in his rear-view mirror, still standing on the step.

Bud pulled into the parking lot of the cafe, pleased that his hunch had been right and that Wanda was in no obvious danger.

Hopefully nobody but he and Gary knew who Scrapper really was, pierced ears and all, though he had no idea why Wanda would want to be incognito. He hoped it didn't have anything to do with George Mills' death or the dino dig, but he somehow suspected it did.

CHAPTER 22

Bud sat in the back booth of the No Delay Cafe, drumming his fingers on the edge of the green plastic table, wondering if he really had any musical talent as he waited for Ray to come and wait on him.

He tried a few bongo-type rhythms, but his fingers were soon tangled up and the rhythm lost—lost just like Wanda had been until he figured out she was really Scrapper. He was a bit disappointed in how long it had taken him to catch on, given all the clues right in plain sight.

Bud drummed a bit more, then stopped. He decided his talents were more in the realm of photography, not drumming. He wondered about the photo show up in Price that Howie had mentioned, and he suddenly felt a bit nervous.

Maybe he should adopt a sort of pen name for his photography, like writers sometimes do—maybe something like Ace or Ansel.

He took his pen and notepad from his pocket and started practicing writing it in different flowery styles—Ansel Shumway—over and over. He liked the way it flowed, and he decided to sign his photographs that way. He then started feeling a bit pretentious and put the paper and pen away.

Now Ray was standing there, waiting to take his order.

Bud said, "Howdy Ray. Got anything with meatballs in it?"

Ray answered, "Nope. Sorry, Bud. You asked me that last time you were in here, if I remember right. If Wanda was here, she could whip something up."

Bus replied, "Well, how's about a hot roast beef sandwich?"

"Anything to drink with that?" Ray asked.

"A cup of coffee with cream," Bud replied. "Sure is a lot quieter in here today."

Ray replied, "Yeah, and a good thing. I was about to lose it with all the racket and hecticity. Was kind of like being in a can of fishin' worms."

Bud laughed. "Where'd everybody go? Back to Colorado?"

"No, last I heard, they're out searching that area around the petroglyph panel down in Buckhorn Draw."

"Searching for what?" Bud asked.

"Well, you know, whatever UFO lunatics search for. Little green men, parts that fell off space ships, mysterious circles burned in the grass. They also told me they're going to find Wanda."

"Find Wanda in Buckhorn Draw?" Bud asked.

"I guess, if she's there."

"Take my word for it, she's not there."

"You sound like you know something, Bud," Ray replied soberly.

Bud hesitated, then said, "Ray, I got a call from Wanda this morning. She sounded like something might be a bit haywire, but yet I think she's OK—for now, anyway."

Ray eased himself into the booth, across from Bud. He looked tired and harried.

"Bud, do you have any idea what could be going on? I sure as heck don't." He looked defeated.

"No, Ray, but I intend to find out."

"But that's not even your job, since you're not the sheriff anymore," Ray replied. "And just between you and me and the bedpost, I kind of doubt if the new sheriff is gonna figure anything out. Where is he, anyway?"

"Well, I'm not sure, but you know, Ray, he has an office to take care of there in Green River. There are lots of other things going on."

Bud thought about asking Ray about George Mill's death, then decided against it. He added, "I know he's concerned about Wanda, but we don't really have any signs of foul play, so for now, she's simply a missing person case. But I have a hunch she'll show up sooner than later."

Ray stood back up, shaking his head, then said, "Well, you sure sound like you know something I don't know. I hope you're right. I'd like to get rid of her irritating cousin, not to mention have her back."

With that, he turned and went into the kitchen, just as Bud saw a red Jeep pull up outside the cafe. A short somewhat stocky older man got out, and he looked to Bud like someone who had spent their life in the outdoors. Bud figured this wasn't anything unusual, as everyone out here looked like that, mainly because there was nowhere else to spend your life around here but outdoors.

The man came into the cafe, nodded in greeting to Bud, then sat down in a front booth where he could see out the big window. He seemed to be watching for someone.

Since Howie wasn't here to discourage it, Bud decided to go talk to the fellow. He went to the front booth.

"Howdy," he said. "Name's Bud Shumway. Mind if I join you for a minute while my food's cookin'?"

The fellow looked surprised, but was congenial enough. Bud sat down, not really sure what to say next. Finally, he said, "Say, I saw you out here yesterday, and I don't mean to interfere with your private business, but you seemed to be following me. I have that FJ outside." Nothing like getting right to the point, he thought.

The man now looked surprised, like he'd been caught red-handed doing something he shouldn't. He stammered for a minute, then managed to say, "I live in Price and was just out looking around. Didn't mean to follow you, though I do kind of recall your vehicle ahead of me for a spell— what I could see through the dust, anyway."

"OK," Bud said slowly. "Like I said, I don't want to invade your privacy, but you were sure right on my tail for someone just looking around. What was that all about?"

Bud was feeling a bit put off by the guy, now that he remembered how close he'd been tailing them.

"Well, I'm Colton Bryant, call me Colt, and I didn't catch where you're from?"

"Green River. I'm a melon farmer down there," Bud replied. He was now getting the feeling Colt wasn't going to tell him anything, but he decided to ask anyway, "You involved with that UFO bunch by any chance?"

Colt laughed and took off his straw cowboy hat, revealing thick short gray hair. "No, I didn't know there was a UFO bunch out here. Was a UFO sighted or something?"

Bud sighed. Colt seemed congenial enough, but he sure wasn't going to let the cat out of the bag as to why he was following Bud and Howie. Ray was now there, taking Colt's order.

"I'd like a hamburger, no onions, well done, please," Colt said. Ray went into the kitchen, and several of the UFO bunch now came in and sat down.

Bud said quietly, "That's some of them right there. From Colorado. No idea what they're looking for."

Colt studied them for a moment, then said, "Well, maybe they saw that meteorite that blew up the other night and thought that was something from outer space. Of course, it was, but probably not the kind of something they're looking for."

He continued, "Say, I lost a meteorite out here. It's pretty unlikely anyone found it, but if you hear anything, would you give me a call? It's worth some cash, and I have a $1,000 reward out for it."

Bud replied, "Lost a meteorite? How do you lose a meteorite?"

"It was on the seat of my Jeep, and I think I accidentally knocked it out when I was getting my rock hammer and stuff out."

Bud replied, "That's a lot of money for a reward. This thing must be worth some cash, huh?"

Colt replied, "Yes, it is. It's a very rare type, and I had just received it in the mail. I can't believe I was so careless, but I had a lot on my mind. It has extra-terrestrial materials that may hold some clues to the formation of the solar system."

Bud sat for a minute in shock. This had to be Howie's meteorite, the one he and Maureen found and thought was from the fireball they'd seen. The odds of them finding it were slim, but it also raised the question of what Colt was doing, as it had been found near the stock tank and thus the coordinates.

Bud was now beginning to suspect Colt was looking for the dino dig, which kind of seemed to be the most popular activity of the day, for some reason. But why was this guy carrying expensive rare meteorites around?

"Can you describe it?" Bud asked, wondering if it would fit the same description as Howie's. Colt described it, and sure enough, it did.

Just then, Ray sat Bud's lunch on the table at his back booth, so Bud got up to go.

"Why don't you give me your number in case I run into any signs of that meteorite?" He would take the guy's number and let Howie decide what to do.

Bud wrote the number down in his little pocket notebook, then said, "Well, Colt, it's a pleasure to meet you, but next time you're out there and we get in your way, just honk, and we'll let you pass on by."

Bud smiled and touched his hat, then went back and ate his lunch, savoring every bite of the thick gravy and overcooked roast beef, wondering what Wilma Jean was planning for dinner, though he wasn't sure that he wanted to know.

He was proud that he'd managed to stave off starvation as long as he had, and he wondered why Howie hadn't called him yet.

CHAPTER 23

Wilma Jean must've known Bud was thinking about her, because just as he stepped out of the cafe, she called.

"Yell-ow," Bud answered.

"Hon," she said, "Have you seen Howie today?"

"No, and I haven't heard a word from him, either. What's up?"

"Well, Maureen's looking for him, and he's not answering his phone. He's got the office phone patched over to the State Patrol, and they don't know where he is either."

Bud replied, "Well, I bet he's out doing something, maybe out helping Old Man Green, out some place where there's no cell service. I wouldn't worry about it unless he doesn't show up for dinner."

Wilma Jean replied, "I know, but Maureen's dying to tell him the news."

"What news?"

"They got a paying gig, their second one. Their first was your uncle Junior's wedding over in Paradox. This is a wedding over in Elmo."

"I'll be darned," Bud grinned. "That is big news. Say, speaking of dinner, what's on the menu for tonight?"

"It's a secret," Wilma Jean answered.

Bud groaned. He hated secrets. Especially since he had a hunch it was probably going to be an unpalatable secret.

"C'mon, Hon, you can't do that to me. I need to know ahead of time so I have something to look forward to. My life gets pretty boring out irrigating all day."

Wilma Jean laughed. "I know you're not out irrigating all day. Barbara said she saw the FJ parked in front of the No Delay Cafe as she came by from Price. I hope you're not there eating something you shouldn't. You'll never lose weight if you continue to eat like you used to."

Bud started feeling a bit petulant. Wilma Jean knew how important having a good meal was to him. He had to build up his energies so he could think properly, do his job, not to mention all the stuff he had to do to help Howie out. He started clicking the clicker in his pocket.

Finally, she said, "All right. We're having split pea soup with homemade pita bread. You'll love it."

Bud didn't know what to say, but he finally got out, "What about dessert?"

"That's even better. I have a new recipe I'm going to try. You take sliced apples and peaches and drizzle Splenda on them—that's a natural sweetener—then you make a crust out of red pepper hummus. It bakes up really nice and crispy."

Bud finally said, "That sounds delicious." He wondered if white lies were considered a violation of one's marriage vows.

Wilma Jean laughed, then said dubiously, "I bet it does. But I gotta run, Hon. If you see Howie, tell him to call home, like ET."

She hung up, leaving Bud standing on the steps of the No Delay Cafe. He still had no idea what hummus was and decided he needed to check it out before things went any further. How did he know it wasn't toxic in large quantities?

Maybe that's what had killed George Mills—his wife feeding him too much hummus until his heart gave out. In any case, Bud was beginning to give up on ever having that spaghetti and meatballs he'd been craving.

He now noticed Colt watching him from the big front window, and he tried to hide his disappointment, wondering when this vegetarian kick would end—soon, he hoped. In the meantime, he was also wondering where Howie was. For some reason, he had a hunch that he might be out at Buckhorn Draw with the UFOers.

Bud was soon on the Green River Cutoff, and when he got to the cliffs where the dino dig was, he noted someone was once again following him. There was no one up at the dig, which was good, and as Bud took a sharp corner on the road, he could see through the dust behind him. It was Colt in his red Jeep, and he was right on Bud's tail.

This irritated Bud, and he thought of stopping, but what if Colt wasn't really following him? He'd find out soon enough when he took the Buckhorn Draw turnoff.

He passed the old cabin and can dump, noting that the white Ford pickup was parked there and someone was walking around as if looking for something.

Sure enough, as he took the turnoff, Bud could see the Jeep still following as he began the descent into the canyon. Before long, he noticed the dust was thicker and thought he could see two vehicles back there. It finally dawned on him that the white pickup had also joined the adventure.

Bud sighed. He didn't like this one bit, having strangers follow him and having no idea why. He thought about heading on out to Jackass Flats and trying to ditch them on the rough four-wheel road, but that might not be as easy as he'd like, since they were both also driving four-by -fours.

He continued on down the canyon until it curved around and came to a fenced-in area between the canyon wall and the edge of the road. He was at the Buckhorn Petroglyph Panel, a lengthy stretch of rock art from the long-ago Barrier era of several thousand years ago. There were several cars in the parking area, but Howie's Land Cruiser wasn't among them.

Bud stopped and got out. Might as well go take a look. He'd been here numerous times, but didn't have his nice Canon until recently, so maybe he could get a few good photos. Besides, he would then know if the two vehicles were following him by whether or not they also stopped.

He walked through the gate in the wooden fence that protected the petroglyph site, noting a small group of people at the far end of the panel. Bud stopped and stood under a couple of big petroglyphs that were painted on the redrock in rich shades of dark rust.

The figures were upwards of four feet tall and stood with their arms outstretched. Their torsos were wedge-shaped, with thick shoulders and thin hips, and one had horns on its head, while the other's head was square like a block.

Bud composed some photos, enjoying himself. He wished he was retired so he could get out and do photography whenever the mood hit him, even though summer on a melon farm wasn't bad, he had to concede. His boss, Professor Krider, was visiting family in Texas, and other than a little irrigating, Bud really didn't have a lot to do.

Finally, the small group came over to Bud's end of the panel, and he could hear them talking. He soon surmised it was some of the UFO bunch. They were looking at a long group of small figures that trailed across the rock face.

"See," one guy said, "This is proof that early humans were visited by aliens. Check out the antennae on that little guy at the end."

"Right, Dewey," another said. "As usual, you're just jumping to conclusions with no scientific basis at all. I personally think it shows that early humans were aliens."

Now someone else piped in, "I think these are just early cartoon strips."

Dewey now said in a dramatic voice, "You have to align with the protocols to pass through the inter-dimensional doorway. And you must be careful to not disclose too much of what you know."

"Were these early aliens illegals?" Someone else asked, ignoring Dewey, then continued, "You know, these things are very thought provoking. You first wonder if they were graffiti, but then you realize they're works of art. What are they trying to tell us? And why here?"

Now the group stood in silence, pondering the rock art. Bud noted that both the Jeep and the pickup had stopped at the parking lot, and the drivers had gotten out and were talking to each other. Before long, they both got back into their vehicles and returned the way they'd come. Bud wasn't sure if they'd been following him or not, but he was glad they were gone.

Bud took more photos, the afternoon sun lighting up the rock art perfectly. He was glad he'd decided to come on out here, though he really didn't know why. Just something to do, he supposed, and look for Howie.

Now one of the UFO group said in an alarmed voice, "Where's Lillian?"

Dewey answered, unconcerned, "I dunno."

Another asked, "Has anyone seen her since our last stop? Did anyone see her get in the car?"

"I didn't," said a voice. Now everyone seemed a bit panicked, trying to recall where they'd last seen her.

"Last I saw her was over by those dinosaur tracks we found in that little side canyon. You think she maybe didn't get in and we thought she did?"

"Obviously," Dewey said. "We need to go back and get her. Hopefully, she's been abducted by a UFO in the meantime."

"That's a terrible thing to say, Dewey," someone said. "We should call the sheriff."

"There's no cell service in here," Dewey said, still unconcerned.

"She either got out at the dinosaur tracks or at the bridge when we stopped there, but I don't remember seeing her there."

Bud watched as the group quickly ran and got back into their cars, hightailing it back down the draw towards the bridge, which crossed the San Rafael River a few miles ahead.

He wondered how they could possibly leave one of their party behind, then decided they weren't your typical Earth dwellers, but were rather more focused on things of a higher order.

He decided to follow along and see what happened. If Lillian really were missing, his expertise with search and rescue and as former sheriff might come in handy, especially since it appeared the real sheriff, Howie, was nowhere to be found.

CHAPTER 24

Bud followed the group for several miles to where Buck-horn Draw opened up and an old swinging bridge crossed the slow and muddy San Rafael River. The bridge had tall cement pillars at each end.

The UFOers parked over in a nearby small camp-ground, but Bud parked his FJ by the bridge and walked over to one of the pillars. A metal sign attached to the ce-ment pointed out that the bridge had been built in 1937 by the CCC (Civilian Conservation Corps) and was 167 feet long. It was now used for foot traffic only, as a newer and sturdier bridge had been built nearby.

Bud knew that this bridge had been responsible for cre-ating access to this northern part of the San Rafael Swell, a huge and wild uplift crisscrossed with slot canyons and impressive stone monoliths. The road now crossed the river and continued on up to Interstate 70, a good 20 or more miles away.

It was the only road that bisected this rugged country, and if Lillian truly were lost, it was a very serious proposi-tion, especially for someone who was probably not familiar with survival techniques.

Bud looked around a bit, but there were tracks every-where. He backtracked onto the road they'd just come down, but the gravel surface showed nothing but vehicle tracks, and if Lillian had headed back towards the petroglyph panel, they would have surely seen her walking down the road.

She had to have been left back where they'd found some dinosaur tracks, though Bud had no idea where that would be, as he'd never heard of tracks in this area.

The UFOers were walking around everywhere, yelling for Lillian and making a lot of noise. Bud knew that she would hear them if in the general vicinity. He started walking down the road in the opposite direction they'd come from, looking for tracks. Had she mistakenly thought her group had gone ahead towards the freeway and headed that way?

He could see Bottle Neck Peak looming above the road ahead, a huge sandstone spire hundreds of feet tall, and he wondered if she might have wandered over towards it to get a better look. But he found no tracks.

Now the group were back in their cars and, seeing Bud, they stopped and informed him that they were going to go on down the road to the dino tracks to look for Lillian. Bud followed as the group turned down the Mexican Mountain Road, which headed pretty much east, dead-ending some dozen or so miles ahead above the river. There, if the water was low, one could hike down a mile or two to the Mexican Mountain airstrip, a primitive runway for bush planes that set beneath the huge ramparts of the red cliffs of Mexican Mountain.

If Lillian was walking down this road, she was getting farther from civilization, not closer, even though it might look like it was headed in the right direction, back to Green

River. But deep canyons and high cliffs blocked any hopes of passage.

Bud followed the cars at a distance so as to not eat too much dust, and he could soon see the huge sandstone walls of Window Blind Peak across the river. The huge butte stood above the desert floor like a giant undulating curtain drawn across a window, thus its name.

He wondered how someone could possibly think the Mexican Mountain Road was a way out, as it seemed obvious to him that the road had to end at some point, given the huge cliffs in the distance.

Maybe Lillian hadn't noticed, but it was more likely she had and had veered off in the direction of the upper Swell, knowing that I-70 wasn't all that far away, but not knowing that the deep and treacherous Black Box would block her path.

Now Bud noted an airplane in the distance, and it appeared to be the same one he'd seen yesterday. It looked like it was again scouting for something, and he suspected it was Cherokee Smith.

Bud finally caught up with the UFOers where they'd stopped at the mouth of a small canyon. No Lillian, and they were now starting to get panicked.

They decided to go on back to the bridge and look some more, leaving Bud behind. He would continue on down the road for a few miles just to make sure Lillian hadn't headed that direction.

Bud stopped several times and looked for tracks, with no luck, and was beginning to fear the worst, that Lillian had indeed veered off the road and headed cross-country. It was now getting on late afternoon, and Bud worried that she would get totally lost in the dark.

He was soon near the end of the road and could see a vehicle ahead, parked at the small parking lot where the road ended. He thought he recognized the vehicle, but hoped not. But as he got closer, he realized his fears were correct.

It was the Emery Country Sheriff's Land Cruiser—and Howie was nowhere to be seen.

CHAPTER 25

Bud got out of the FJ and began searching for Howie's tracks, hoping to get an idea of where he had gone. He finally found them, and they led straight to the river, down a long slope and a good mile away. He could see the airstrip in the distance, on the opposite banks of the San Rafael.

It was late spring, and with a good snowpack in the high country, the river was carrying a big load, deep and narrow with its banks saturated and unstable, as well as full of quicksand. There was no way Howie could cross it and get to the airstrip, if that was his destination.

Bud got out his binoculars and climbed a small rise so he could see better. He glassed the countryside, but saw no one. He forgot about Lillian for the moment, deciding to follow Howie's tracks, thinking maybe he was sitting in the cottonwoods near the river where Bud couldn't see him.

It was downhill all the way and didn't take Bud long to reach the river, where, sure enough, Howie's tracks went right down the bank and seemed to just stop there.

Bud glassed the other side of the river, but there was no way Howie could've crossed the river. It was impossible, at least without a boat of some kind.

Bud was puzzled. He wondered what Howie was doing way out here in the first place. It was out of character for him, as he wasn't a seasoned outdoorsman like Bud and seemed to have a hesitancy to go out into these wild places alone.

Bud started yelling, but his voice just echoed off the cliffs and came back around to him, empty sounding and alone. He now thought again of Lillian, noting the sun was now getting fairly low in the afternoon sky. It would soon be evening. He needed to do something, but he wasn't sure what that something should be.

He began walking along the river bank and finally found the tracks again and followed them back to where they came out on the road about fifty feet from Howie's Land Cruiser, then disappeared. Bud now noted additional tracks on the road, tracks from a vehicle that looked to have smaller and narrower tires.

Bud now pulled his little notebook from his pocket and left a note under the Land Cruiser's windshield wiper, telling Howie to call home. It seemed futile, but at least it was something.

He got in the FJ and started back down the road the way he'd come, and he could soon see the airplane again, now cruising fairly low, not far off. He watched it, wondering again what it was doing.

Before long, he was back near the canyon the group had stopped at, and he pulled over and parked. He put on his jacket and made sure his Ruger was loaded and safe in its shoulder holster, then grabbed his small day pack, which held water and a few survival items, such as matches and gorp.

Bud began searching, looking for Lillian's tracks, and sure enough, he found tracks that were smaller than a man's. The soles had a light tread, which would be typical of someone not wearing hiking boots, but shoes suited for an urban setting.

He tracked them for a few hundred feet, then lost them as they veered off the road. Picking them up again, they went straight towards a small ridge. Now Bud suspected Lillian was trying to head towards the freeway.

Only problem, Bud thought, was the freeway was some 20 miles distant, with the Black Box between here and there. The Black Box was a 600-foot deep canyon carved by the San Rafael River into dark Precambrian rock, and there was no way anyone could cross it.

Now he could hear the plane again, and it was soon not more than a couple of hundred feet above him, but quickly disappeared over the ridge. Bud wished he could communicate with it somehow, as it would make finding Lillian much easier.

He began hiking faster and was soon on top of the small ridge, and sure enough, could see a small figure in the distance below him. He yelled, but the figure was too far away to hear him.

Bud began a slow jog, but before long his side started hurting, and he had to resume walking. Wilma Jean was right, he thought, he needed to lose a few pounds and get back in shape. Sitting on a tractor hadn't done him much good in the aerobics department.

Now the plane was buzzing who Bud thought must be Lillian, and the figure turned and looked back. Bud waved his arms again, and now he could see the figure doing the same. It turned and headed towards him.

Bud waited, and in about fifteen minutes the figure had reached where he stood, but it wasn't at all who he expected to see.

It was Howie.

CHAPTER 26

"I sure didn't expect to see you out here, Sheriff," Howie said, huffing and puffing as he leaned against a big rock. "Man, you scared me at first—I had no idea who would be following me way out here."

"Well, I think you surprised me as much as I did you. I was expecting you to be Lillian, one of the UFO people. She's apparently lost out here."

"Lillian?" Howie asked with surprise. "I thought it was Wanda."

"You thought who was Wanda?" Bud asked, puzzled.

"Who I was looking for," Howie answered, a bit impatiently.

"I didn't know you were looking for anyone," Bud said. "Is that what you're doing running around out here?"

Bud and Howie just stood and looked at each other for a bit, then Howie said, "You know Sheriff, I think this is how aliens must feel when they try to communicate with us Earthlings."

Bud was confused, so he tried again. "So, Howie, I take it you somehow thought Wanda would be out here heading cross-country straight for the Black Box? And then you decided to come and check it out for yourself, way out here in the middle of nowhere like this?"

Howie thought for a minute, then replied, "Yeah, I guess I kinda walked the dog with an empty collar on this one. I knew something was wrong when I got out there a ways. Kind of my typical MO, I guess—that stands for Modus Operandi, you know." He looked chagrined, though Bud had no idea why and was even more confused.

Howie then asked, "But what are you doing out here, Bud?"

Now the plane circled overhead, then waggled its wings as if trying to tell them something. The sun was beginning to dip behind the distant cliffs, and Bud was again wondering if Lillian weren't out there somewhere.

Bud sighed, then said, "Howie, let's start from the beginning. Tell me why your Land Cruiser is parked back by the end of the road and how you came to be way out here."

Howie was now excited and acted like he didn't hear Bud.

"Sheriff, look, it's Cherokee, and we agreed that if he found Wanda he'd wiggle his wings like that, then head in her direction. She's out there, just as I thought, and we need to find her before it gets totally dark. This is serious stuff, Sheriff. What should we do? She could die out here." He paused, then added, "And so could we, I guess."

Bud was beginning to form a theory.

"Howie, did you see someone out there and then take off after them, thinking it was Wanda?"

"Why else would I head out into this wild country in the middle of nowhere, Sheriff? You think I'm that crazy that I'd just take off like that?"

Bud sighed again, then replied, "OK, how long ago did this happen?"

"Well, I was up flying with Cherokee and we saw Wanda down there, and she looked totally lost. She started waving at us. I knew I had to do something, Sheriff, so Cherokee landed on the road and I headed out after her. But I totally lost her, and that's when I saw you. Actually, I thought you were her, and she'd somehow circled around behind me."

"You were flying with Cherokee?"

"Yeah, he came and picked me up. I thought I could meet him at the Mexican Mountain Airstrip, but when I got there and saw the road ended on the wrong side of the river, he took off and landed on the road and picked me up."

"Took off and landed?"

"Howie was beginning to sound impatient. "Yeah, he was at the airstrip, where I'd agreed to meet him. You know, the one over by..."

Bud interrupted, "It's OK, Howie, it's starting to make more sense. But we need to find this missing person. So Cherokee is saying he sees them out there by waggling his wings?"

"Yeah, and it's waggling, not wiggling, I guess. I sure don't know much about this aviation business like you do, Sheriff, but yes, that's what we agreed on."

Bud wasn't sure what to do at this point, although things were beginning to become clearer, but only barely. Lillian was indeed out there, heading straight for the drop-off at the Black Box, and the way things were going, it would soon be dark. If she decided to keep going after dark, she was certain to just walk off the sheer edge into the 600-foot depths of the canyon. They needed to do something quick.

"Howie, why don't you carry on in the direction the plane's saying to go, and I'll try to sweep around to the left in case she veers that way. I have a feeling she thinks she's headed for Green River."

"And what should I do when it gets dark, Sheriff?" Howie asked. "I left my flashlight in the Land Cruiser."

"Just turn around and head back to the road, then stay there and wait. I'll eventually come back and find you. If you can't find the road, just stay wherever you are and don't wander around. We don't need another person lost out here."

Howie nodded his head in agreement and headed out, then turned after going a few steps and asked, "What if it's Wanda instead of Lillian?"

But Bud had already taken off at a brisk walk. He would cut across at an angle towards the Black Box, then hike back towards Howie along the rim, providing there was enough light to see where he was going. That way he would maybe intercept Lillian if she decided to try to strike out towards Green River instead of the freeway.

Bud hiked as quickly as he could, and it wasn't all that long that he could feel a great depth ahead of him, even though he couldn't yet see it. He instinctively knew the deep chasm was nearby, and he felt a sense of dread.

He'd stood on the rim of the Black Box before, and it had left him feeling dizzy to see the river far below. It was different from other river canyons because of the dark rock, which made it feel mysterious and even deeper than it actually was, and it was very narrow. And now the evening shadows made everything seem even more mysterious.

He was now at the edge of the canyon, and he carefully began angling his way back towards Howie. An evening breeze rose from the chilly depths. Bud stopped and listened for a moment. He swore he'd heard a voice.

He strained to listen, but there was nothing, and now the breeze had died down as the sun set. The Black Box became even more deadly feeling, and Bud stepped back further from the rim and started walking once again towards where he knew he would eventually meet up with Howie.

He stopped again. This time, he knew he'd heard a voice. It was a woman's, and it sounded like it was coming from the depths below.

It was his worst fear come true—Lillian had fallen into the abyss.

CHAPTER 27

Bud stood, straining to hear the voice, but it again died out. He wasn't sure what to do at this point, as there was no way he could scale into the depths below, even if it were Lillian. About all he could do was to try to figure out where the voice was coming from and then go for help. It seemed like a somewhat futile plan, but he again began trying to hone in on the location of whoever was calling.

It was nearly dark at this point, and Bud called out, then was silent, waiting for a return call, but heard nothing. Now he could once again hear something, and it seemed as if the voice was coming more from ahead. This gave Bud hope that maybe Lillian hadn't tumbled into the canyon, but was instead maybe rimrocked on its edge. He began slowly moving forward, careful to watch where he placed his feet, staying back from the jagged rim.

He stopped every so often and listened carefully, but the sound seemed to have stopped. He started feeling a bit spooked by the darkness and the nearby depths, and he wondered if Howie were being careful, although he figured he was, given his innate caution.

Bud then began thinking about how wild and isolated this country was and of all the times he'd spent out here when he was sheriff, looking for people who'd gotten lost or injured.

The San Rafael Swell was an unforgiving place, and he'd had more than his share of adventures out here. Sometimes it seemed as barren of life as Mars must be. He'd been out here at night when the sky was so thick with stars it would take your breath away, and even though he'd never been one to think much about life on other planets, he didn't doubt it was possible.

Bud now stopped and listened, noticing how dark it had become. Black clouds had shrouded the western sky within the last half hour or so, blocking out the waning sunrays that had provided a bit of light, and he wondered if a storm was moving in.

It was rapidly getting pitch dark, and the last thing he wanted was to get lost out here, or worse yet, have Howie lost. Bud could take care of himself, but he wasn't so sure about his ex-deputy.

Now he thought he heard the voice again, calling, but it seemed even farther in the distance, yet it seemed weird, as if it was getting closer and closer. Bud stood, trying to figure out what was going on, as the voice seemed to take on a thicker and yet shriller sound, almost as if it were several voices at once, all tangled up together.

A chill went up his spine, and Bud's imagination began running away with him as the sound got closer and closer. Was there really something to this alien thing? Normally, he wouldn't think twice about it, but out here alone, in the dark, with this strange noise—he began to feel more and more uncomfortable.

He had just decided to return to the FJ and see if Howie was there when it happened—the air above him was suddenly filled with a shrieking that made him drop to his knees in fear and surprise, nearly dropping his flashlight, a shrieking that seemed to close around him with a strangeness that seemed otherworldly.

Bud went for the Ruger in its holster, but it was all over before he could even get it out, the sound gone into the night. He remained on his knees for a bit, then burst out in laughter, both from relief and from the irony of it all.

A small flock of Canadian geese had come straight up from the waters in the Black Box and flown right over Bud's head, scaring the bejeebers out of him. Normally, he would've immediately recognized what was going on, but he'd prepped himself for aliens and other high strangeness, so his mind was on another track, one he normally didn't travel.

He laughed at his own reaction, then stood, relieved. He decided to head back to the FJ, but as he turned to go, he again heard the voice calling—but this time, it sounded like two voices, and one sounded familiar.

Bud angled along the edge of the dropoff a bit further until he finally could hear better.

Someone was yelling, over and over, "SOS! SOS! SOS! Mayday! Mayday!"

And then, after a pause, he could hear the same voice calling, "Bud! Bud! Help!"

It had to be Howie. Bud now rushed, as quickly as was prudent, further along the edge until he came to the source of the voice. He leaned over the edge a bit and shone his big flashlight down into the depths.

There, sitting on a small ledge, legs dangling precariously over the edge, sat Howie, holding for dear life onto a small bush that grew from a declivity in the cliff. And someone was sitting by him, also barely on the ledge, holding onto Howie for dear life, about to pull him on over, and that someone looked to Bud like a small woman he'd seen in the state park named Lillian.

Bud stood in shock, not sure what to do. He was well-trained in search and rescue, but that training usually included having a few tools at his disposal for such rescues, things like ropes and other people to help out.

This situation looked to him like it could go south any moment, long before he could get back to his FJ and grab his tow strap or whatever he could find to facilitate dragging the pair back up the cliff. He no longer carried high-angle rescue gear with him, now that he wasn't sheriff, and Howie's Land Cruiser, which would have rescue equipment in it, was way down the road.

"Howie, hang on. Whatever you do, don't let go. I'll think of something ASAP," Bud said, though he wasn't sure what that something could possibly be. He could hear Howie repeating his advice to Lillian.

Bud was beside himself. How in hellsbells was he going to get this pair back up the cliff? He wasn't strong enough to just pull them up, and besides, he couldn't reach Howie.

Bud knew that the first tenet of rope rescue was to have a rope. He grimaced, trying to think of something that could substitute, but couldn't think of anything. The second tenet was to make sure the person being rescued was stable and safe so they couldn't fall. He had no idea how he could do this alone and with no tools.

Now Howie was yelling again, "Sheriff!"

Bud leaned out over the edge. Howie continued, "We're coming up. I think if I can get around to where Lillian can stand on this bush where I can push her up, you can reach her."

Bud lay down on the edge of the cliff, not sure what to say. It was risky, but he didn't have a better plan.

"OK, Lillian," Howie said, now standing on the ledge while still holding onto the bush. "Keep hanging onto me, and as I move over under the bush, grab it. Once you get a good hold, I'll hang onto your waist as you stand and start to climb up, using the bush as a step, OK?"

Bud held his breath as he shined the light on the bush, trying to light the way. He could see Howie taking slow tiny steps along the ledge as Lillian moved with him. Soon she had a good hold on the bush, sitting where Howie had been, then she climbed up onto the bush. It wasn't a very large shrub, and Bud hoped it would hold.

Bud leaned over as far as he dared, and he soon felt Lillian grab his hand. He then began slowly pulling himself backwards, away from the cliffs, bringing her with him.

Howie was trying to help push her up from below, but his own position was so precarious he couldn't do much, so Bud knew it was mostly up to him. Fortunately, Lillian was small and light, and he soon had her up and over.

She lay there, puffing from the exertion, then finally moved away from the edge. Now Bud concentrated on helping Howie, not sure if he could hoist him up like he'd done Lillian, as Howie was larger and weighed more.

Howie grabbed onto Bud's arm, but Bud was having trouble pulling him up. He could feel himself starting to slip, but now Lillian had grabbed his feet and was holding on for dear life. Bud worried that all three of them might go over, but Howie was finally able to use his feet to help climb, cramming the toes of his leather boots into cracks in the rock face until he was finally up and over.

They all lay there for a moment, then stood up. Bud shone his flashlight on Lillian, and she looked white as a sheet, but otherwise OK. The light showed a big grin on Howie's face.

Howie asked, "What exactly does SOS stand for, Sheriff? I was wondering that the whole time I was yelling."

Bud answered, "It means Save Our Ship or Save Our Souls, depending on if you're in a ship or not."

"Well," Howie replied, "You sure did a good job of saving our souls, for sure, Sheriff."

Lillian spoke quietly, looking straight at Howie. "And thanks to you, he was able to do that. If you hadn't come along when you did to keep me from going off the edge, I wouldn't be here right now. You saved my life."

Howie just stood there, apparently trying to absorb what she had just said as Lillian hugged him.

CHAPTER 28

Bud sat at his old desk in the Emery County Sheriff's office, pushed back in the chair with his feet up, even though it was now Howie's desk. Bud thought of the many times he'd come in to find Howie in that same position, reading old detective magazines from the free bin at the library.

He was glad he was a farmer and no longer had the stress of the sheriff's job, but he was also a bit worried about his ex-deputy, as Howie seemed to be talking more and more about leaving the job to become a musician, and Bud wasn't so sure one could make it in the music industry when they lived in a remote desert town in Utah. Shoots, it was hard enough when you lived in a place like Los Angeles, or so he'd heard.

Howie now pushed the front door open with his foot, his arms full of drinks and sandwiches from his old drive-in across the street.

"Oh man, Sheriff," Howie said, "You're gonna love this new sandwich I came up with. They made it special for us. It has roast beef, pickles, mayo, hot mustard, and pepper jack cheese, with white chocolate and almonds on top, though I had to get the chocolate and almonds from the store. It's going to be really tasty, kind of a sweet and sour thing, or maybe more like spicy instead of sour."

Bud was eager to try it out, even though it sounded a bit questionable. He hadn't had anything to eat yet except a green smoothie Wilma Jean had made, and this time she'd stood there and watched him drink it.

He'd felt it was a sad state of affairs when his wife treated him like a little kid, but he wondered if maybe he'd been acting like one, not taking care of himself. But now that the after-effects of all that had worn off, his appetite was recovering, and he was hungry for some real food.

Bud took a big bite, then shook his head appreciatively.

"Not bad at all, Howie," he said, feeling a bit guilty for eating it, wondering if he was developing an eating disorder. "You've created another culinary miracle."

Bud had heard that foods that have the same color have the same amount of calories, and thereby the green pickles must be the same as spinach, and the white chocolate, mayo, and pepper jack must be equivalent to mushrooms, and so on. He decided that his favorite food, vanilla bean ice cream, was also white, so it must also have the same calorie count as mushrooms, a theory that made him feel a bit better.

Just then, the phone rang, and since Bud was sitting next to it, he answered.

"Sheriff's office, Bud speaking."

The voice at the other end asked for Howie, so Bud gave him the phone. Howie was soon nodding his head and saying nothing, listening, then after awhile said "Thanks" and hung up. He looked at Bud with a surprised look on his face.

"What's up?" Bud asked.

Howie shook his head as if trying to shake some sense into it.

"I can't believe it, Sheriff."

"Can't believe what?"

Bud started his countdown. One-thousand one, one-thousand two...

Howie just sat there in disbelief, until Bud reached one-thousand seven, then he answered.

"That was the lab up in Salt Lake. They found poison in George Mills' body."

Bud sat up straight. "Poison? No kidding?"

"Yeah, it surprises me, too, and I'm the one who suspected it in the first place," Howie answered.

"What kind of poison?"

"It's called aconite. Ever heard of it?"

"No," Bud answered. "Aconite. What did they say about it?"

"The lab guy said they'll mail the report, which has more info, but it's an alkaloid. It's very poisonous and can be detected only by sensitive toxicology equipment. The person poisoned stays coherent up to the end, so sometimes it looks like a heart attack, as it shuts the heart down first, and one of the symptoms is tingling of the fingers. He said it's the perfect poison for murder because it's hard to detect. Sheriff, I was right, someone poisoned George."

Bud was shocked. George poisoned? Why would anyone poison George?

"I'll be darned, Howie. Last night you became a hero, saving Lillian and all, and today you're proving to be another Hercule Poirot."

"Who's that?" Howie asked.

"He's a famous detective from Agatha Christie novels."

Howie beamed, "Not bad for a ten-cent brain, eh?"

"Did you tell Maureen about the rescue last night?"

"Well, I just told her we'd found a missing person. I try to not toot my own horn too much, Bud. You know, I really don't want her to think I'm high on myself."

Bud replied, "Well, Howie, I don't think that's a problem with you. You don't go around like that. In fact, it might be good if you did tell her more about how well you do your job—and folks like Ray, also."

"Oh, I do, I do. Like when I helped Old Man Green find his missing steers, I told her all about that later."

Bud frowned. Finding Old Man Green's missing steers was nowhere on the same level as rescuing someone hanging off the edge of a cliff. Maybe someone should start tooting Howie's horn for him, if he wasn't going to do it himself, at least where Maureen was concerned.

They sat for awhile, munching on the sandwiches, until finally, Bud asked, "How did you end up flying with Cherokee yesterday? Was it fun?"

Howie's eyes lit up.

"Oh man, Bud, it was like nothing I've ever done. It was incredible. I'm thinking it would be great to get a license—I could fly the band around to our gigs, if we ever get any."

"Did Maureen tell you about the gig in Elmo?"

"What gig?"

"She didn't tell you?"

"No, by the time I took Lillian back to the state park and all, Maureen was in bed. And she was in a big hurry this morning cause she was a bit late for work. And I think she was mad at me for getting in so late. We got a gig?"

"You did," Bud replied.

"The wedding?"

"I assume so. Who's getting married?"

"I dunno. Some gal named Alberta. I don't think she's from Elmo," Howie replied. "The guy lives there, but I don't know his name."

Howie continued, "Well, that's good news. One more step closer to fame and fortune. Anyway, I got a call from Cherokee, asking if I wanted to go flying. I said sure, but he was at the Mexican Mountain strip and wanted me to meet him there."

"Good Lord," Bud answered, "Why not just fly to the airport and pick you up? Why drive clear out there? And you can't drive to the strip anyway."

"Yeah, I found that out. He wanted me to bring him some hydraulic brake fluid and a GPS."

"Brake fluid? Man, this guy sounds like an accident waiting to happen. And why a GPS?"

"He said his GPS quit working, and since I was coming anyway, maybe I could be copilot and help him look for something. He didn't say what. I had to go clear out to the airport to get the brake fluid, it's a special aviation mix. He hiked over to the river and I threw him the fluid, almost landed in the river, then he took off and picked me up there on the road by where I parked. We flew around a bunch. Man, was it exciting. He flew really low, looking around, and I operated the GPS. He'd give me bearings and we'd go figure out where they were."

"What was he looking for?" Bud asked.

"Well, Sheriff, I don't know, I was just happy being a copilot. I had no idea it was that easy, just climb into the plane. I thought you needed a lot of training. He even let me fly the plane a bit!"

Bud tried to be patient. He tried again, "But what was he looking for?"

"He never did tell me. I just assumed it was some kind of recon flight, you know, like in those old World War II movies, except there wasn't no war so it wasn't as scary."

Bud sighed. "Well, OK. I'm really glad you got to go up, Howie."

Howie replied, "If I hadn't, we would've never seen Lillian. I saw her out there, heading straight for the Black Box, and I got Cherokee to let me off there on the road and I went after her."

"That was a really good thing to do, Howie. You saved her life."

Howie was now quiet, as if the reality of it was finally sinking in.

"I guess so, Sheriff. Maybe it kind of makes up for what else I did."

"What else you did?"

"Yeah. I got to talking, and Bud, I was just so excited, and Cherokee, he managed to get out of me where the dig we found was. We flew over it, and now he knows. I think I screwed that one up, Sheriff. I guess I need to stay closer to home." Howie looked grim.

Bud felt his heart sink. He'd suspected that was what was going on, and now he knew he was right. Cherokee had to be involved with a black market bone digger, and the stakes here must be high for someone to be willing to spend money flying a plane around, searching. Planes and fuel weren't cheap.

Bud wondered who Cherokee's client was—and how was George involved, had he known too much? Had Cherokee poisoned George and then left him to die there under the tree?

Maybe it was time to call someone up at the museum and tell them what was going on so they could get down to the dig and set up shop, but Bud didn't want to put anyone in jeopardy. And he still wasn't sure how this tied into the claw and the letter, and he wanted to find out.

He felt a strong urge to click the clicker in his pocket, but managed to instead rub the bridge of his nose. He finally got up to leave.

"Well, thanks for the sandwich, Howie. It was really good. I guess I'll survive one more day. I'm going to go home and get on the internet and see what aconite is."

"Do you mind if I stop by later?" Howie asked.

"Not at all. And don't be hard on yourself about the dig. You know, Howie, life is a do-it-yourself project, and that's how you learn, by getting out and doing stuff, getting experience. Unfortunately, guys like Cherokee are good at manipulating people."

"Yeah, especially ones with TCB syndrome," Howie replied glumly.

"What's that?"

"Ten-Cent Brain."

Bud walked out the door, leaving Howie to pity himself all alone.

CHAPTER 29

Bud sat in his easy chair, reading about poisons on his laptop computer. He'd read about the most deadly poisons known to humans, with antifreeze and hydraulic brake fluid being pretty well up on the list, but aconite wasn't there.

He searched some more, then finally found a reference:

"Aconite is a plant indigenous to many parts of the world. All parts of this plant are poisonous, but the root is the most highly toxic. A half tablespoon of a tincture of aconite root placed in a bottle of whisky is enough to kill a very large man. Placed in a drink, the alcohol goes unnoticed. Aconite has been called the perfect poison to mask a murder. It can be detected only by sophisticated toxicology analysis using equipment that is not always available to local forensic labs. In some cultures it is called the Queen of Poisons."

Bud leaned back in his easy chair, kicking the footrest up. Pierre was snuggled down next to him, his long lean body stretching almost the full length of the arm, and Hoppie lay on the floor at his feet. Both were full of some ham that Wilma Jean had cooked for them. Bud once again felt a bit slighted, glad he'd eaten a sandwich earlier.

So, aconite was a bad poison, Bud thought, but where did Cherokee get it, if he was indeed the one who poisoned George? It didn't seem like something one could just pick up at the store. And once again, what was his motive? George's wife didn't know anyone named Cherokee, so he and George probably hadn't been friends.

Bud continued reading:

"The neurological features of aconite poisoning can be sensory (numbness of face and limbs), motor (muscle weakness in the limbs), or both. The cardiovascular features include chest pain, palpitations, tachycardia, and fibrillation."

No wonder everyone thought George had a heart attack. He had the symptoms, but that wasn't what had actually killed him.

Bud fiddled with the clicker in his pocket, accidentally waking the dogs. Hoppie jumped into his lap, wanting to see what the noise was. Bud stroked the Basset hound's silky ears.

"No, Hoppie, it's not one of your little squeeze toys. You don't wanna know what this is, little buddy. It's your mom's idea of trying to civilize you guys, but so far I've managed to hide it well enough that she seems to have forgotten about it."

Hoppie licked Bud's hand, then settled down in his lap. Bud set the laptop aside. He was sleepier than usual, and he figured it was the combination of sweet and sour on the sandwich, or maybe it was because he was stuffed to the gills.

He should get up and make some coffee, he thought, but the chair was just too comfy, and he didn't want to disturb Hoppie and Pierre.

Before he knew it, Bud was soon fast asleep, twitching and snoring with the dogs.

Now, somehow, he woke, and things seemed different and very strange. He didn't know what to make of it, but the house was filled with a thick mist that floated through the windows and doors, even though they were closed and it had been sunny outside before he'd nodded off.

He sat for a moment, thinking it must be smoke, but it didn't smell like smoke at all. It must be foggy outside, something that occasionally happened when the weather was just right, as they lived not all that far from the river.

Bud got up from the chair, waking the dogs in the process, deciding he needed some coffee to wake himself up, as he had to still be dreaming. Even if it were foggy outside, it wouldn't come into the house like this. Something was wrong.

He stumbled into the kitchen, barely able to see where he was going, and started some coffee in the percolator pot. It started making its tell-tale percolating hisses and bloops as he made his way to the sink and splashed cold water onto his face, trying to wake up while the fog seemed to get thicker.

And now the percolator sounds were getting louder and louder, until they sounded like something huge outside hovering over the house, something really big that hissed and blooped, until finally the sound seemed to enclose the house and make Bud want to cover his ears.

He could now make out a weird blue light through the windows that lit up the thick fog both inside and outside the house.

He was beginning to feel really uncomfortable, like something was very wrong, and he decided to call Wilma

Jean. He pulled his cell phone from his shirt pocket, but it was dead.

Now Bud could see the kitchen door opening, and a strange white light came through it with a shining figure at its center. It was Lillian!

She was now motioning for him to follow her, to go outside where that strange noise was coming from, with that strange blue glow. Was this the same thing that had hovered over the No Delay Cafe, the glow that Ray had seen? A chill went down Bud's back.

He didn't want to follow Lillian, but he had no choice. It felt like a big tractor beam from some science-fiction movie was pulling him out through the door, and he was helpless. He followed her like an automaton.

They walked slowly into the front yard, and Bud could now see that the strange glow was coming from a weird craft that was indeed hovering over the house.

It was unlike anything Bud had ever seen and looked like an oblong thick cigar with drumsticks attached to it. It reminded Bud of what some little kid would draw, yet it sent a cold terror through him.

And now the space craft was landing right by him and Lillian! He wanted to run, but his feet were frozen in place.

The craft's door opened and a set of stairs magically emerged, going all the way to the ground, some twenty feet or more. Bud knew what would happen next—it would be just like some weird 1950s space movie—an alien would emerge and come down the stairs, an alien with a big round head and long thin arms and legs.

Sure enough, an alien exactly like that emerged and came down the stairs. Bud could now feel himself shaking, and he wanted to run. But Lillian didn't look a bit concerned, in fact, she had somehow acquired a big bouquet of beautiful blue and purple flowers, just like the ones George had planted in his garden.

Now the alien had reached the bottom of the stairs and walked forward a bit, holding its hand up just like the dirt bikers had, in greeting. Lillian stepped forward to meet it and handed it the bouquet.

The alien looked pleased, and Bud was now suddenly relieved, thinking it hadn't come to harm them after all. It held the flowers to its nose as if to sniff their fragrance, but something strange then happened—the being began to look just like George.

Bud was horrified at what happened next. The alien suddenly began to shrivel until it looked like a balloon with the air gone, then what was left poofed into nothingness, the flowers falling to the ground.

Lillian looked shocked, and now the space craft had also begun to fade into nothingness, into the mists and fog. Lillian turned to Bud, dumbfounded, saying over and over, "I didn't mean to kill him. I didn't mean to kill him," then she, too, faded into the mists.

Bud woke in a cold sweat, Hoppie still on his lap and Pierre at his side, sleeping. The house had no fog inside, in fact, Bud could see the warm sun coming in through the big living room windows.

It had all been a dream.

He rubbed his eyes, trying to wake up. That was the last time he would eat white chocolate with hot mustard and pepper jack. Maybe Wilma Jean's diet plan wasn't such a bad idea after all.

CHAPTER 30

Bud just sat there for awhile, thinking. He'd had dreams like this before, and he knew they were his subconscious trying to get through to him that he knew something he didn't know he knew.

What could the dream have possibly meant? Was Lillian somehow involved in George's death? That seemed un- likely, but had he and Howie overlooked some important evidence? And why would an alien turn into George?

Bud got up and started the percolator pot, half expect- ing to see a blue glow outside, but everything seemed normal. He let the dogs out into the yard for a bit and wan- dered around outside with them, looking at Wilma Jean's flowerbeds.

No blue and purple flowers there, just some white daisies that had managed to winter over from last year, and some pink and white petunias that Wilma Jean had planted.

He want back inside and poured himself some coffee, sitting at the kitchen table and sipping it, wishing he had some vanilla bean ice cream to put in it, but it was all gone. And about all that was in the fridge besides rabbit food was some red pepper hummus. It looked like he was maybe going to have start doing some of the grocery shopping, the way things were going.

He got up and looked in the Scooby Doo cookie jar his sister had given him for his birthday a few years ago, but it was empty. He picked up the bag of Barkie Biscuits on the counter and looked at the ingredients. They weren't too bad, but he then decided that they were a no go as they smelled too much like dog biscuits. Things were looking pretty desolate on the goodies front.

He sat back down in the big chair and picked up his laptop. He suspected Howie would be coming by soon, and there was one thing he needed to do first.

He keyed the phone number Colt had given him into the internet search engine. He already knew from the prefix that it was a Price number, but he wanted to see if he could tie it to anything else.

Sure enough, the number came up for the small college there. He decided to try his luck and see if Colton Bryant was by chance affiliated with the museum or perhaps the geology department, so he pulled up the college's main page, then searched through the list of professors.

No Colton Bryant. He must be affiliated with the museum, thought Bud. He himself had been through the museum numerous times, in fact, it was one of his favorite places to go, and sometimes Wilma Jean would drop him off there while she went shopping. Bud especially liked the paleontology part and the huge mastodon skeleton that dominated that wing.

Bud decided the best way was to just dial the number and see if anyone there knew Colton Bryant. The phone rang, then a voice answered, "Bone Lab, Wilt speaking."

"Say, I'm looking for a fellow named Colton Bryant. He gave me this number. Is he around?"

Bud could hear Wilt yell, "Anybody here named Colton Bryant?" He was soon back on the phone. "Nope. Nobody here by that name. In fact, nobody here at all but me and some guy named Harry."

"Well, is he sometimes there? Does he work there?" Bud was puzzled. Maybe he'd written down the wrong number.

"I dunno. Let me ask Harry. Hang on."

Bud could hear muffled talking, as if the guy had his hand over the receiver. He was soon back.

"Would that be Colt?" He asked.

"Yeah, that's it, Colt," Bud replied.

"Well, next time, ask for Colt, not Colton. No, he's not here."

"When is he usually there?" Bud asked. Given the terse nature of whoever he was talking to, he didn't figure he'd get much information, but he decided to try anyway.

"I dunno. Let me ask."

Bud was confused. Why would Wilt have to ask? Bud had been in the Bone Lab, it was where the museum stored the numerous fossils it acquired through digs or through trade with other museums. He knew they had an extensive collection, but he also knew there was really only the lab director and a few volunteers who worked there.

More muffled talk ensued, then Wilt was back.

"Look, I'm just the janitor, and I only come through here a few hours a week. Nobody around here knows diddlysquat, just me and a volunteer. He says Colt's gone. You need to call back later."

Wilt hung up the phone.

171

Bud was back to square one—no, back to square zero, he thought. But at least he now knew that Colt was somehow affiliated with the museum, which meant he was maybe more trustworthy than Bud had originally thought. And Colt obviously knew the guy who was in the white state pickup following Bud and Howie, so maybe there wasn't anything illegal going on from those two.

Maybe—or maybe not. They could both be involved in illegal bone hunting, and it wouldn't be the first time professionals had done something a bit illegal, crimes that were millions of years in the making, so to speak.

Bud recalled the case of the T-Rex named Sue, which now sat in the Chicago Field Museum of Natural History. Sue was named after her founder, and had been the center of much legal controversy as to who her rightful owner was.

The bones had been confiscated by the FBI in a raid, but were eventually purchased by the museum for over eight million dollars. No one had actually done anything illegal in that case, as it was more a matter of who owned the bones, since they were found on land leased from the government.

But Bud knew that many paleontological remains had been illegally dug from federal and state lands and sold into the black market for large sums of money, removing possible scientific finds from ever being known.

He himself had often found scrap dino bone out in the badlands near Green River, but he always just left it where he'd found it, except for a time or two when he'd called the museum, thinking it might be something important.

But he'd never been involved in anything of significance, though he suspected the dig he and Howie had just found might qualify. And someone else thought it was important also—whoever had sent that letter with the claw in it—who was just maybe the same person who had been illegally digging and trying to cover their tracks.

Did they have anything to do with Colt? Bud didn't think so, as someone affiliated with a bone fido bone lab wouldn't be slinking around trying to cover their tracks. In fact, Bud suspected Colt was looking for the same thing he and Howie had happened to stumble upon, the bone site, though he had no idea how Colt would know about it.

Speak of the devil and he appears, Bud thought, looking up to see Howie's Land Cruiser coming down the lane. He suspected that Howie wanted to go back out to the No Delay Cafe and see what they could figure out—and maybe that would include determining who would want to kill George Mills via an obscure type of poison that was hard to come by.

He wondered how Cherokee Smith fit into all this. Somehow, Bud suspected the rogue pilot had the answers he and Howie were looking for.

CHAPTER 31

Bud and Howie sat in the back booth of the No Delay Cafe, eating lunch while listening to Ray moan about the lack of business. It appeared that the UFO group hadn't been around after the incident with Lillian. Howie had told Bud that he'd seen them earlier, driving out to the geyser, so they were still in the area, at least.

Bud figured they must be college students out on a lark, as school would now be out for the summer. He hoped their sense of awareness had improved, as he wasn't into another search and rescue endeavor.

Bud interrupted Ray's complaining to ask, "Say, Ray, you got any fry sauce?"

"You bet," Ray answered, getting up and going to the kitchen and returning with a small dish of thick pinkish-white sauce. "I make my own," he said as he put the dish down by Bud.

Bud tasted it, then asked, "What's in this, anyway? Everyone I ever ask says it's a secret recipe, available only in Utah."

"Can't tell you," Ray replied. "It's a secret recipe."

Howie grinned, then said, "I made it when I had my cafe. I'll tell you what's in it. It's one part ketchup to two parts mayonnaise. You can substitute barbecue sauce for ketchup."

Ray groaned. "That's like a magician telling someone how to do the magic trick. You've just violated the venerated and most secret guild of fry-sauce makers, my friend."

Bud laughed. "Whatever's in it, it sure is tasty, especially on ribs. But speaking of ribs, Ray, do you have any idea about any bone digging around these parts? Heard any talk about such?"

Ray frowned. "Bone digging? You mean illegal dinosaur bones? Black market stuff?"

Bud answered, "Yeah, illegal digging. Has anyone mentioned anything to you that might be a clue to something going on?"

Ray sat down in the booth next to Howie. "You guys think something's going on?" He paused, then added, "I do recall something, maybe. Remember that guy who I told you seemed suspicious, the guy in the white state pickup? Well, he was sitting here the other day talking to another fellow, a guy who drives a red Jeep, and they were talking about dino bone. Those two are about as suspicious as you can get in my book."

Howie asked, "What exactly did they say?"

Ray looked at Howie. "I dunno, nothing much. They were just talking about different kinds of dinosaurs. Most of it was over my head, stuff about clades and all those Latin names, you know, like Utahraptor. I dunno, maybe Utah's not so Latin, but I bet raptor is. Stegosaurus and Jurassic and other stuff too, like the proper tools to dig with, that kind of thing. Then one of them got a phone call, and they both took off like bats outta hell."

"Where'd they go?" Bud asked.

"Beats me. Towards the Cutoff Road, I guess," Ray replied. "Drove like it was the end of the world, TEOTWAWKI. One of them mentioned something about a Cherokee Indian as they were walking out. You know, I've heard you can make good money selling stuff in the back rooms of the Tucson Rock and Gem Show, but there's money, and then there's the wrong kind of money. But I gotta get back in the kitchen and do some prep work. Haven't seen hair nor hide of Scrapper this morning. I appreciate you boys coming by."

Ray stood and went back into the kitchen.

Howie had finished his hamburger and was staring vacantly out the window. Finally, he asked, "Sheriff, what's TEOTWAWKI?"

"The End Of The World As We Know It," Bud replied.

Howie looked perplexed. "That's a weird thing to say, don't you think, Sheriff?"

"I dunno," Bud answered. "He's probably been listening in on the UFO guys. That's something they would maybe talk about."

"Speaking of UFOs," Howie said, "I forgot to tell you."

Bud waited, starting his countdown. Finally, at one-thousand ten, he gave up and asked, "Oh?"

Howie replied, "Glad you asked, Sheriff. I never know if you're really interested in this kind of stuff or not. But I kind of followed the UFO bunch this morning for a ways out to the geyser, just to make sure they didn't get lost again."

Bud replied, "Well, the geyser's a pretty well-marked tourist thing, Howie, so they'd probably be OK. But what happened?"

Howie replied, "Well, you know that old corrugated steel building there by the road, just before you turn to go to the geyser, you know, the intersection that goes on out to the old missile base?"

Bud tried not to feel impatient. He answered, "I do, and?"

"Well, that building itself was actually part of the missile base at one time, something to do with munitions, but now it's in pretty bad disrepair. It's a shame seeing all that cool old stuff falling down. Anyway, there was a car parked in front of it. You know what I mean, the old missile site from the 1960s where they shot off the Athena and Pershing missiles to White Sands for tests. I like that kind of stuff, Sheriff, so I've been out there looking around some. It's pretty dated junk by now. I actually found an old Pepsi bottle out there from the 1960s and an old insulator."

Bud waited a bit, then asked, "What kind of car?"

"Whattya mean, what kind of car?"

"The one you saw at the old building?"

Now Howie leaned across the booth and whispered, "It was a tan Crown Vic, and I saw Scrapper sitting in it, waiting. I betcha anything that Gary guy, the really suspicious one, he was inside. What would he be doing in there, Bud? It's got holes in the walls. I would've gone and peeked in, but Scrapper would've seen me."

He continued, "But there's more. When I was taking Lillian back to the state park last night, she told me they'd been out near there the night before, looking for UFOs, when they saw lights inside it."

"That's odd," Bud said. "Was she sure? There's no electricity out there."

"She swore by it, Sheriff. She said it freaked everyone out and they left. That old missile base is a strange place at night, with all those old buildings, and to see strange lights inside...and she said someone came out and looked around with a big searchlight like they were guarding it."

Bud rubbed the bridge of his nose, wanting to click the clicker in his pocket, but restraining himself. Lights in the old missile base building? Someone guarding it? Scrapper sitting outside in Gary's car?

"Well, Howie," Bud finally said, "Maybe we should get on out there and see what we can find. It seems suspicious to me."

"Yeah," Howie replied. "Everything seems suspicious any more to me. Maybe it's the aliens' way of preparing us all for TEOTWAWKI."

He looked at Bud and grinned as they paid the bill and walked out the door.

CHAPTER 32

Bud and Howie cruised through the town of Green River, Bud noting Wilma Jean's big pink Mary Kay Lincoln Continental and Maureen's VW Bug parked in front of the Melon Rind Cafe.

Bud and Howie had first gone up to Gary's trailer, but no one was home, though Bud noted the dogs were in the yard, which he thought odd, as he knew Gary took his dogs everywhere he went. This made Bud feel unsettled, and combined with what Ray had said about Scrapper missing, he began to think something was wrong.

They then headed on out the old road that led to the geyser and also the now defunct Green River Missile Base, once known as the Utah Launch Complex Annex of White Sands.

Bud knew that the missile site had been extensive, and old buildings lined the top of the Mancos shale hills as one came into town from the east, though the actual launch site itself was on the other side of the freeway on top of a distant hill.

He'd been out at both sites a number of times, poking around through the old buildings and tall towers, trying to figure out what everything was.

They pulled up in front of an old corrugated steel building that had a classic 1960s look with its silver metal exterior and weathered front door and a sign that read, "Contractor Closed Area by Order of Site Director."

It was the second of three such buildings, all about a tenth of a mile apart and on down the road from the main launch site, and Bud had noted the first one they'd passed had an old sign that read, "Range Communications Station Charlie 401." In front of both were weathered no-trespassing signs hanging half off their posts.

The building looked like it had been abandoned for many years and like a good wind would blow it over. Tumbleweeds formed a dreary-looking pile where they'd blown up against one wall, and the tin siding had been stripped off by the winds along that same side, leaving several rusted holes.

Sure enough, Gary's old Crown Vic sat there in front of the door, but no one appeared to be around. Bud and Howie cautiously walked around the side of the building and peeked in through a big hole about the size of Hoppie.

It took awhile for their eyes to get acclimated to the dark interior, but the building looked empty except for a few old upside-down cans of some kind, along with some smaller tumbleweeds that had apparently made it in through the gaps in the walls.

Neither Bud nor Howie said anything as they stood there and tried to see inside, half expecting someone to be in there. Bud was about to give up on finding anything of significance when Howie whispered, "Hey, Sheriff, look over in that far corner. It looks like a workbench and some kind of tools on it. We need to get inside to check it out."

"Agreed," Bud answered. "And I'm worried about Wanda. Ray said she didn't show up this morning, and it's odd that Gary's car is here."

Howie replied, "Wanda? I thought he said Scrapper was missing."

"They're one and the same," Bud replied, "But don't tell anyone."

Howie looked at Bud in surprise. "One and the same? How do you know that, Sheriff? You mean Wanda's not really missing?"

"Well, she is now," Bud answered.

"I'm confused," Howie sighed. "But what's new?"

Howie was now trying to crawl through the hole, his long legs first, and it appeared he was actually going to fit. He struggled for a bit, then was in.

"Being tall and skinny does have its advantages, I guess," he said. "I'll go and open the door."

Bud was soon inside, and he and Howie went over to the bench they'd spotted.

"What's this white stuff everywhere?" Howie asked.

"I'm not sure," Bud answered, "But look here, Howie."

He handed Howie a small object he'd just picked up from the floor under the workbench.

Howie whistled. "A claw! Just like the one I got in the letter."

He now looked around nervously. "Sheriff, maybe we'd better get out of here. It feels really suspicious."

"Agreed," Bud replied, smelling some of the white stuff. "But I have a hunch I know what this stuff is."

"What is it?" Howie asked.

Bud ignored him, pretending to be examining the workbench closer.

"Well, Sheriff, what is it? You're keeping me in suspense."

Bud started counting. One-thousand one, one-thousand two...

Now Howie was getting impatient. "Sheriff, it drives me nuts when you do this..."

Bud grinned, then spat a bit on his finger, getting some of the white powder wet. He then made it into a small ball.

"Just as I thought, Howie."

"Thought what?" Howie said, now even more impatient.

Bud replied, "It's pretty much certain."

"Is it some kind of drug, Bud?"

"Howie, if it were a drug, they're sure wasting it. It's all over the place."

Howie was now openly frustrated. He himself now made a small ball of the stuff, then smelled it and started to taste it, then changed his mind. He grinned, looking knowingly at Bud.

"It's Plaster of Paris, isn't it, Sheriff?"

"Well, you sure figured that out in a hurry," Bud answered. "Gypsum."

Howie looked pleased with himself, then said, "Let's get out of here. I have a bad feeling about this place. But why would there be Plaster of Paris in here? You suppose they used it for missiles somehow? Maybe they made casts of the missiles before they wrecked them so they could rebuild them again." Howie was now wandering around the building, looking at everything.

"Wrecked them?"

"Yeah, old Jimmy Zussman, I heard him telling somebody down at the Melon Rind that he'd found one of the missiles over on the Swell. Guess they crashed as many as they got to White Sands."

"Well, that may be a bit of an exaggeration, Howie, but I do know they crashed a few. There's one down in Canyonlands National Park, over by the Maze. Saw it myself a number of years ago."

"No kidding?" Howie remarked.

"But to answer your question, Plaster of Paris is used for casts to encase dinosaur bones for transport," Bud said. "This appears to be a staging area for someone digging bone and taking it elsewhere. Bone looters come in and take museum-grade specimens out and sell them, and the bones disappear into private collections and are lost from science forever. It's a dirty profession."

Howie was now back over by Bud, examining a cigarette paper he'd just picked up.

"Say, you haven't been drinking, have you?" Bud asked.

Howie was surprised. "Me, drinking? You know I don't drink, Sheriff, well, not alcohol, if that's what you mean. I think what you're smelling is this. Whoever was smoking this was the one drinking, is my guess."

He handed the cigarette paper to Bud.

"Tequila," Bud said. "But it's not from someone drinking, it's a tequila-scented roll-your-own paper."

"I had no idea there was such a thing," Howie said in surprise. Another clue, is my guess, but a clue to what I can only guess."

Howie paused, then added, "Say, Sheriff, I came up with what I think is the winning name for Wilma Jean's bowling alley."

"What's that?"

"Tumbleweed Alley."

"Shhh! Did you hear that noise?" Bud asked.

"What noise?"

"It's coming from over there—that door looks like it goes into an office."

Bud and Howie cautiously walked to the back of the building and looked in through the doorway, where they saw a figure on the floor, moaning.

"It's Scrapper," Howie said.

"Yup, it's Wanda alright," Bud answered, kneeling beside her. "And she appears to be in a world of hurt."

CHAPTER 33

Wanda was now sitting up rubbing her head, and Bud was trying to decide whether or not to call the EMTs or take her himself to the Green River Medical Clinic. Her fake beard stubble was all smeared, the makeup rubbed off on her collar.

"Are you OK?" Howie asked.

Wanda tried to stand up, mumbling, "Thank God you're here. We have to find Gary. They took Gary. I tried to stop them, and they whacked me on the head..."

She then collapsed back down into a sitting position, Howie hanging onto her.

Just then, Bud held up his hand, telling Howie not to talk.

He whispered, "There's someone out front. Stay here and be quiet."

Bud quietly slunk back into the main building and along the wall, stopping by a hole where he could hear better, though he couldn't see outside. There appeared to be several people out front.

Now he heard a voice.

"Why do gullible people always think every unidentified light in the sky is aliens? People are so superstitious. That had to be a meteorite."

Bud thought he recognized the voice, but he wasn't sure.

"No, it was actually somebody's lost luggage, from 10 years ago," a second voice said.

"Anyway, if it was a UFO, the military would have already shot it down and stolen the technology and dissected the bodies so they could extract DNA to build a super race of humans," the first voice said.

Now Bud was sure he knew who it was. It sounded just like Lillian.

The second voice said, "They already did that. They're those big pro-wrestlers on TV."

Lillian ignored the second voice, who Bud decided must be Dewey. She continued, "I wish they'd quit saying everything was hovering lights. It's like saying flying saucers, so 1950s. But I don't think we should go in here, you guys, it says no trespassing."

Bud hurried to the front door and quickly opened it.

"Welcome to Area 51," he said in a deep Twilight Zone voice. The UFO group almost started running, then just stood there in shock.

Bud continued, "Come on in, we need some new blood." He laughed, then continued, "But say, you guys, we need your help, and thanks for the tip, Lillian. We came out here and found Ray's wife, Wanda—you know, from the No Delay Cafe. She needs a ride muy pronto into the clinic. We need to go find her friend, who's missing. Can you guys take her in right away?"

The group rushed into the old building and were soon helping Wanda to their car and on their way to the clinic. It happened so fast Bud hardly knew what had hit him.

Now he and Howie were back in the Land Cruiser, and Howie had a look on his face of both excitement and fear.

"Sheriff," he said, "Wanda told me they have Gary and are trying to make him tell them where the Therizinosaur site is."

"Who's they?" Bud asked, watching the UFO group's cars heading towards town in a cloud of dust.

"I dunno. She kind of quit talking, said her head hurts. I guess she'd been laying there for awhile."

"That's bad news, Howie. I mean, about her head, but also about Gary. I hope he's OK, but how do they know about the Therizinosaur site?"

"I'm thinking Gary was the one who sent me that letter," Howie replied, turning the Land Cruiser towards town.

"Say, Howie, stop," Bud said. "I have a hunch—I don't think Gary took them to the same site we know about. I mean, think about it. If Gary knows about the Therizinosaur site on the Cutoff Road and is the one who sent you that letter, why would he tell whoever conked Wanda on the head about it?"

"Maybe to Save His Soul," Howie replied. "I bet he was threatened. After all, they conked Wanda, which wasn't so nice."

"I think he would try to stall them, because that site has some kind of major significance, and he wouldn't reveal it except in extreme circumstances."

"Wouldn't being threatened be an extreme circumstance?"

Bud replied, "Well, for you and me, maybe, but from the looks of Gary's teeth, he's been in a few fights, and I don't think he would cave in that easily. He'd be more likely to take them out on a wild goose chase, and I think I know where that wild goose might be hiding."

"Wild goose?"

"There's a quarry down by the geyser. It's supposed to be a big secret, as the paleo guys don't want anyone looting it. It's called the Suarez Quarry, and they found a new species of dinosaur there, the Geminiraptor suarezarum. It was named after the Suarez sisters, who found it. They're twins, thus the Gemini in the name. That's how I can remember it so well."

"Wow," Howie said. "What does it look like? That would be cool, to find a new species."

"If I remember right," Bud replied, "It was a seven-foot-long raptor-like dinosaur with large eyes and dexterous claws and is pretty old, about 125 million years. But if Gary knows this country like I think he does, he knows where that quarry is and will take the guys there as a diversion from his real discovery, which is the one with the coordinates on the Cutoff Road. Turn around, Howie, and let's head the other way."

Howie turned the Land Cruiser around and they started on the road to the geyser. They cruised on for a bit, following the road down through a series of badland cliffs.

"Why are there so many dinosaur bones around here, Sheriff?" Howie asked.

"Good question, and I'm sure not a geologist, but I enjoy reading about this stuff. This is an area where the formations from the days of the dinosaurs are like an open book. In some places, they're still covered by other formations, but the Colorado Plateau is really unique in that it's slowly rising, and these sedimentary layers are exposed through erosion—like the Morrison, which is called the

Dino Boneyard. And where we found the dig, up by the Cutoff Road, that's all Cedar Mountain Formation, which is also a good one for dinosaurs. The Cedar Mountain is like a big river stretching from Price on over into Colorado, and it's full of dino bones."

They were now winding down the dirt road through the very formations Bud was talking about, leaving a rooster tail of dust behind them.

"Wow, Sheriff, you sure know a lot more about it than I do. But hey, I wrote a song about all this alien stuff. Wanna hear it?"

"Sure."

"You sure?"

"Sure, I'm sure, Howie."

"OK, here goes. It's sung to that old Sons of the Pioneers song, 'Ghost Riders in the Sky.'"

An old sceptic went riding out one dark and windy day,
Upon a ridge he rested as he went along his way,
When all at once a big convoy of weird spacecraft he saw,
A-plowing through the ragged sky and up the cloudy draw.
Their tailpipes were on fire and their bodies made of steel,
Their exhaust was black and shiny and the atoms he could feel,
A bolt of fear went through him as they warp-sped through the sky,
For he saw the Aliens coming fast and he heard their mournful cry.
Yippie yi yaaaaay,
Yippie yi ooooooh,
Ghost Aliens in the sky.

"Anyway, it goes on and the skeptic gets told by the aliens that he has to mend his disbelieving ways. There's more, but you get the idea."

Bud laughed. "It's great! Are you gonna play it at the wedding?"

"Geez, I dunno. Do you think it would be appropriate?"

"Well, not for a wedding itself, unless it's an alien wedding, but it would be fun at the reception. Isn't that what you're playing for?"

"Yeah, you're right."

"It'll be fun. But don't look now, Howie, we're being followed. And not by just that state pickup, but also the red Jeep. Looks like a regular convention coming up."

CHAPTER 34

They neared the geyser, where Bud directed Howie to take a left off the main road. He could see the yellow travertine in the distance where the geyser sat on the edge of the Green River.

The geyser's schedule was irregular, and Bud could see that it wasn't currently erupting. It was a rare cold water carbon dioxide geyser that was the result of an oil exploration company drill hole.

They were now going down the Little Valley Road, and the Suarez Quarry was only a few miles away, deep in the heart of some of Utah's best dinosaur bone country. Bud noted that the two vehicles were right behind, not even trying to hide the fact that they were following them.

"How do you know where the secret quarry is, Sheriff?" Howie asked as Bud directed him to make another turn, this time onto a barely visible dirt track.

Bud answered, "Back when I was sheriff, I actually had to come in here to provide backup for a BLM arrest."

"The Bureau of Land Management arrested someone down here? Why?"

"This guy had a piece of land down by the river with a placer gold setup. He was legal, but the road he graded over BLM land to get his heavy equipment down there wasn't so legal. They gave him a pretty reasonable time to fix it back like it was, but he didn't do it. So he got to spend a little time in jail and also pay a pretty good fine."

"What did that have to do with the quarry?"

"Well, after it was all said and done, one of the BLM guys wanted to go check out the quarry, cause it's also on BLM land. So he and I went out to make sure it wasn't being looted. It had been graded over for the season. We didn't find anyone there, fortunately, but today, we may."

"What will we do if they start shootin', Sheriff?" Howie asked.

"Well, if they shoot, we can shoot back, or we can leave and come back with reinforcements."

"I vote ahead of time for leaving," Howie said.

"Yeah, I agree that life's better when it's simple," Bud replied. "Say, Howie, I had a really weird dream, and it was about George being poisoned."

Bud told Howie the dream while Howie listened intently. Howie shook his head, then replied, "Wow, that really is weird. You know, I've been trying to figure out who would poison George, and why, and I haven't been able to come up with anything. I still think it was Cherokee, or he at least knows something about it. Do you suppose it had something to do with all this black market dino bone stuff, Sheriff?"

"Maybe," Bud replied. "But that dream's trying to tell me something, Howie, and I don't know what. Why would I dream that the flowers killed the alien?"

"Maybe flowers are poisonous to aliens. Something to remember if we're ever invaded. Might come in handy."

Bud nodded, then said, "Looks like someone walking

up the road ahead, coming our way. What would someone be doing walking way out here?"

"Maybe it's a hiker," Howie replied.

"Out here?"

"Well," Howie replied, "Those hikers hike all over the place. Ever been to Yosemite? Man, they're thick as bees on honey out there, just everywhere. They carry these big ole walking sticks made out of hickory so they can whack bears on the head. By the way, did I mention that I called Cherokee and asked him why he was flying around? I figured since he'd helped save Lillian, I mean, he's the one who spotted her, that he'd tell me what was going on—sort of like friends would, maybe."

"What did he say?"

"He said 'nunya.' What's nunya, Sheriff?"

"None of your business."

Howie was quiet for a minute, then said, "Well, I'm sure sorry, Bud. I guess I really do get out of hand always asking you questions and stuff. I'll try to tone it down a bit."

Bud laughed. "No, Howie, that's what nunya means, none of your business."

Howie seemed relieved. "You mean nunya means none of your business, not that the answer is none of my business?"

"Last I heard," Bud replied. "But Howie, let's pull over and give this guy a ride. He looks a lot like Gary—either that or it's his brother—and he looks pretty tired."

Howie pulled the Land Cruiser over next to the bedraggled figure walking up the road. It was indeed Gary, and he looked exhausted. Bud reached back and opened the back door, and Gary got in. Bud then handed him a cup of coffee from his thermos. Gary thanked him and settled into the back seat.

"Have you seen Scrapper?" Gary asked.

"Yes, we found her at the old missile site. She's in the Green River Clinic. I think she'll be OK," Bud replied. "What happened?"

"Sounds like you figured out Scrapper is really Wanda. Did she tell you anything?" Gary asked, sipping the hot coffee.

"No, but maybe you should. What was going on?"

"Nunya," Gary said, relaxing back into the seat and closing his eyes. He finished the coffee, then handed Bud the empty cup, then took out a pouch of tobacco and a package of Juicy Jays Root Beer Flavored Rolling Papers and started rolling a smoke, acting like he had no intentions of telling them anything.

Bud turned and looked at Gary, who said, "I got no horse in this rodeo. I need to get home to my dogs."

CHAPTER 35

Bud watched Howie, wondering what he would do. Bud knew that Gary had to know something about what had happened to Wanda, plus he didn't just teleport himself out here into the middle of nowhere.

Howie looked a bit distressed, and Bud could tell he was trying to make a decision. Should he just take Gary home and hope that he could later get Wanda to tell him more, or should he seize the moment and try to cajole Gary into being a bit more forthright with what was going on?

Bud wasn't even sure what he himself would do in this situation, so he was doubly interested in Howie's reaction.

Gary was now smoking the cigarette, trying to blow the smoke out the window, and the faint smell of root beer filled the air.

Finally, Howie pulled out his cell phone and dialed a number, then said, "Cyndie, can you get me the number for the BLM office?"

Bud knew he was talking to the State Patrol dispatcher in Green River. Since the Emery County Sheriff's Office had no dispatcher, the county had an agreement to use the State Patrol dispatch when necessary.

Howie hung up the phone, then punched in a new number. Bud watched Gary out of the corner of his eye.

"Hello. This is the Emery County Sheriff requesting assist for a possible arrest. Can you send a couple of your law enforcement rangers out to Little Valley, ASAP?"

Now Gary looked visibly nervous. Howie hung up, a look of satisfaction on his face. He turned to Bud.

"They just happened to have a couple of rangers there in the office and are sending them right out. Fifteen minutes."

Gary had apparently recovered enough energy to talk. He threw the cigarette out the window and said, "You called the rangers? Who you gonna arrest, and for what?"

Bud knew Howie had no real proof that there was even anyone out here to arrest, other than the theory that Gary had been kidnapped and forced to reveal the quarry site. Howie was bluffing, but Bud knew that Gary didn't know that.

Howie just smiled at Gary, then started humming a song and tapping his fingers on the dash, ignoring him. Bud was impressed, as it was a good psychological trick, one he didn't know Howie had up his sleeve—keep your suspect wondering and maybe he'll get nervous and fess up—except Bud wasn't sure if Gary had anything to fess up or not.

Now Bud noticed that two vehicles were behind them. It was the state pickup and the red Jeep. Gary looked more and more nervous and started to roll another cigarette.

Howie looked at his watch and said, "Ten more minutes."

Gary put the cigarette stuff away and started tapping his fingers on the back of the seat, just like Howie. Finally, he said, "I didn't hit Wanda. I hope you know that."

Howie replied, "No, I didn't figure you would do something like that, Gary. But you know she's going to tell us all about what happened, so you might as well save us the suspense and be first in line to tell the story. Might save the BLM guys from having to speculate and haul you into jail with the bone poachers."

"Bone poachers?" Gary said. "What the heck are bone poachers?"

"You know good and well what they are," Howie answered. "In fact, the BLM will be interested in knowing about that letter and claw you sent me. Your Radium postmark didn't throw me off for one minute."

Bud was impressed. Howie was playing Gary like a pro, just like someone in a detective movie. Bud sat, silent, waiting to see how things transpired, hoping Howie's ploy would work.

CHAPTER 36

Gary sat silent for some time, and Howie finally looked again at his watch. "Five minutes till the BLM shows up."

"Who the heck are these guys waiting behind us?" Gary asked.

Howie replied, "FBI."

Gary groaned. Bud held his arm up to his mouth, hiding his grin. Who knows, maybe the two really were FBI agents, but he doubted it. It seemed more likely they were on the other side of the law, especially if they knew Cherokee Smith.

Howie was gaining confidence and continued with his ruse. He said, "You tell us what happened and where the bad guys are, and we might just forget about that letter, Gary. It's up to you." He again looked at his watch. "Three minutes."

Gary sighed. "All right. All right. They're out at the Suarez Quarry, and they ain't goin' nowhere. You guys won't have any trouble arrestin' them. They're probably walkin' up the road right about now, just like I was."

"How so?" Howie asked.

"I stopped them dead in their tracks. See, they've been digging all over the country and using that old missile base building to hide stuff while they wrapped it for transport.

They whacked Wanda on the head last night when we refused to tell them where the Therizinosaur dig was, the one you have the coordinates for, then they made me show them, threatened to kill me, but I took them to the Suarez Quarry instead. I stuck some rocks in their tailpipe, so now they're walkin'."

"That wasn't so nice. What does that do?" Howie asked.

Bud groaned. Howie's authority act was beginning to go south.

"You never heard of the old potato in the tailpipe trick?" Gary asked incredulously.

"I thought you said it was rocks," Howie answered.

Gary replied, "Anything that will stay up there works, even a banana. It keeps the car from running. When a car's cylinders move up and down, they pull fuel and air in and push exhaust gases out. If the tailpipe is blocked, the exhaust can't go anywhere and stays put in the cylinders, preventing fresh stuff from entering. If exhaust gases can't escape, the engine can't breathe, so it dies."

"Oh," Howie said. "Very clever."

Now Bud decided to intervene. "Gary, how did you get involved with bone diggers in the first place? You mind telling us how you came about knowing where the Therizinosaur site was?"

"I plead the First Amendment," Gary answered.

"It will be easy to match that note with your handwriting," Bud answered. "Might as well tell us now. By the way, you transposed one of the numbers in the coordinates. Took us forever to find the site."

Howie added, "One minute left. I think I see them coming, Bud."

Gary quickly answered, "All right, but you guys have to be lenient here. I realized I had a real scientific discovery, that's why I wanted you guys to find it, turn it in to the right people."

"Why not do that yourself?" Bud asked.

"Because I'd been selling claws on the black market— I'd sold about 30 of those ripping claws. They would put two and two together and arrest me. I just wanted out of the whole deal entirely, and some of the black market guys were following me around, trying to figure out where I was getting stuff, the same guys who've been stealing bone out here, the ones now stuck over at the quarry. They knew it was a major find, a whole new kind of dinosaur and worth big bucks. They were after Wanda, too, cause they knew she knew where it was. I'd taken her out there, trying to get her opinion on what to do, and they knew she was hanging out with me. That was real stupid. That's why she went into disguise as Scrapper, to throw them off."

"Oh man," Howie said. "What a hornet's nest."

"You got that right," Gary replied. "I really had no idea what I was doing, I just wanted to make a little extra money to help out with my vet bills. My dog, Sally, came down with some health problems, and I wanted the best vet care possible for her."

"Is she OK?" Howie asked.

"Now she is," Gary replied. "Except she and my other dog, Max, are probably scared stiff, being left alone. They're a couple of big babies."

"Well, we need to get you home," Howie said sympathetically.

"So that's why you didn't seem too worried about us finding Wanda?" Bud asked.

"Exactly," Gary replied. "Actually, me and Wanda didn't want you looking at all, just a waste of your time. We both felt real bad about that, but you can now see why she was scared. I hope she's OK. Are you gonna arrest me, Sheriff?"

Gary looked desolately at Howie, then added, "I sure don't know what my old dogs will do without me if you throw me in the can. I was dang stupid to ever get involved in something like this in the first place."

Bud looked at Howie, who seemed deep in thought. He didn't envy him having to make this decision. Howie was now looking at Bud, but there was no way Bud was going to influence him on this one. Howie was sheriff, and it was his job, but the law was still the law.

"Well," Howie finally said, "All I know here is what you've told me, and as far as I'm concerned, you could be lying. I mean, what proof do I have that you're not just spinning some tall tale to entertain me until the BLM shows up?"

Gary looked at Bud, confused. Bud shook his head and shrugged his shoulders. It appeared that Howie was trying to find a creative answer to the dilemma.

"Lying to you?" Gary said. "Why would I lie to you?"

"I dunno," Howie replied. "But let me ask you this, what role did Cherokee Smith play in all this, and who murdered George Mills?"

"Cherokee Smith? George Mills? Who's that?" Gary asked, even more confused.

"Tell you what," Howie said. "You help us get these bone poachers, and we'll talk about all this later."

"OK," Gary said. "I'll tell you all I know, but I know my side of all this is going to come up in court, and then I'll be hosed." He looked even more morose.

Just then, two BLM rangers pulled up beside them. Howie got out and talked to them a bit, then the rangers went back and talked to the guys in the two vehicles, who soon left.

The rangers took off for the Suarez Quarry with Bud, Howie, and Gary close behind, eating their dust.

CHAPTER 37

They soon topped a small hill and the rangers pulled over and got out. Bud recognized one of them as the same guy who had originally shown him the Suarez Quarry.

Now the other ranger, who appeared to be the lead, came over to the Land Cruiser and said, "The quarry is just over behind this hill. We want to surprise them, so we're going to hike up above and come around from on top."

The other ranger climbed a small nearby rise and was soon back, reporting, "There's a pickup parked at the base of the cliff, and I can see two guys up there, and it looks like they're digging. We need to be careful, as they could be armed."

"I can tell you for sure they're armed," Gary said, getting out of the Land Cruiser.

Bud wondered if Gary might try to run off, but there was nowhere for him to go in this wild country, and Bud knew Gary was exhausted from trying to hike out.

Howie and Bud got out of the Land Cruiser, and Bud noted that Howie looked a bit scared.

"You fellows need our help?" Bud asked the rangers.

The lead ranger replied, "We're going to sneak up on them, so I don't think so. But why don't you watch from that little rise in case things go south on us?"

"10-4," Howie said, now checking his gun to make sure it was loaded. The rangers took off, staying out of sight of the quarry.

Bud said, "Say, Howie, why don't you go on over to that rock over there, and I'll go to the rise. If they see the rangers, they're likely to try to get away in their pickup and I'll be able to get back over here and cut them off. But if they try to run, they're more likely to head down that draw, and you can keep them in sight from up there. But stay behind the rock so they don't see you."

"10-4," Howie said, heading for the big rock.

"I think I'll stay here in the truck," Gary said. "I ain't much for helping arrest people."

Bud went to his lookout. He could see Gary leaning against the Land Cruiser and rolling yet another cigarette.

Bud watched as the rangers stealthily climbed up the back of the cliffs where the bone quarry sat. It wasn't long before one was on top, above the pair, who were still digging. The other ranger had circled around a bit lower and was now crouching in a small wash, not far from the pair's truck.

But suddenly, the bone diggers stopped digging, looked up, then took off running. Bud couldn't figure out what had gone wrong until he saw a small cloud of dust come off the cliffs. The ranger up on top must have slipped and accidentally rolled some rocks down, alerting the pair to his presence.

Bud took his Ruger from its holster and put it in his jacket pocket, his hand on it, ready in case he needed it.

The pair were running for their vehicle, but just then, Bud could see that the ranger in the wash had started after them, and Bud could hear him yelling something.

One of the pair stopped, putting his hands up, but the other continued running, seizing the moment, as if he knew the ranger couldn't focus on them both at once.

Bud could see the fleeing digger was running directly towards Howie, so he himself started running in that direction, hoping to intercept the man, as he wasn't sure Howie would know what to do. The last thing he wanted was for his inexperienced ex-deputy to get hurt.

But Bud was too slow. The bone digger was obviously in much better shape than he was and was nearing the rock that Howie hid behind.

Bud tried to yell, but he was puffing too hard. Now the digger was almost at the rock. Bud stopped, pulling his Ruger from his pocket, sighting the figure in.

Just then, he saw Howie step from behind the rock, his pistol pointed directly at the startled figure, and Bud could hear Howie command, "Stick 'em up, pardner."

The bone digger put on the brakes and held his hands to the sky, Howie standing there just like Paladin on that old TV show, "Have Gun, Will Travel."

CHAPTER 38

Bud again stood in the irrigation ditch, waiting for the head of water to arrive from the gate he'd opened on up the way. He was happy to be back on the farm where peace and quiet were easy to come by, rather than the hectic life he seemed to have recently fallen into as an unpaid sheriff's deputy, helping Howie.

The previous day had been especially stressful, with the arrests of the two bone diggers, even though he hadn't played much of a part, letting Howie and the two BLM agents do the work while he watched.

The only real trouble they'd had was when they tried to bring the bone diggers' pickup back from the quarry, forgetting that Gary had stuffed the tailpipe with rocks, but they finally remembered and drove it back to town.

Because they'd been able to catch the bone diggers in the act, Gary's role as witness wasn't quite as critical. Bud hoped Gary wouldn't get into much trouble, though by his own admission, the man had been illegally digging and selling Therizinosaur claws.

A small wall of foam came crawling down the ditch as Bud stood there, shovel in hand, enjoying the warm sun on his face. He'd brought the dogs with him today, feeling a bit guilty that they'd been alone so much the past few days, as Wilma Jean had also been busy.

Pierre was now trying to bite the foam as Hoppie lunged at it with his front paws, barking his fool head off. Bud wished he had a video camera—maybe he'd check them out on the internet when he went home for lunch.

Just then, Bud's cell phone rang. He decided that if it was Howie, he'd just let him leave a message. There was no way he wanted to go out to the No Delay Cafe again, as he was ready for some down time. He grinned, happy that he enjoyed his job on the farm. He'd made the right decision when he quit the sheriff's office.

The cell phone rang again, and seeing it was Wilma Jean's number on the caller ID, he answered.

"Yell-ow."

"Hi Hon. Where are you?" She asked.

"Out irrigating. Why?"

"You have the kids with you?"

"I do. They're playing in the water as we speak."

"Oh, I bet that's cute. Say, you coming home for lunch instead of going to the No Delay Cafe with Howie like you've been doing every day? And who knows what you eat there, but I'm sure it's not salad. Anyway, that's not a question, but a command."

"It's exactly where I plan to be, home for lunch," Bud replied. "What's on the menu? Spinach soup with cucumber crackers and carrot juice?"

Wilma Jean laughed, but it sounded a bit contrived to Bud. "Hon," she said, "You just come on home for lunch. I have a surprise for you—no, two surprises—wait, make that three."

Bud groaned. How many times did he have to tell his wife he hated surprises?

She added, "I know you hate surprises, so I'll tell you the big one now. Are you sitting down?"

Bud felt his stomach sink a bit. This must be really big news if Wilma Jean asked him if he was sitting down. He leaned against the irrigation ditch wall a bit, saying yes, then she continued.

"'The results of the Price Love Your Country Photo Contest are now in. First prize went to Jeremy Silver, a senior at Price High School for his photo of the craters of the moon through his telescope, and second went to Annie Bolton of Helper for her photo of a sheepdog herding sheep. Grand Champion is Bud Shumway for his photo called 'The Long Road Home' of a big silver Amtrak engine fading into the sunset.' I'm reading this from this week's copy of the Carbon County Zephyr. Isn't that great?"

Bud was stunned. Grand Champion? His knees felt weak.

"Hon, you there?" Wilma Jean was asking.

Finally, he answered, "Yes, but I just can't believe it."

"Well, I can," she answered. "And you get $50 and a chance for the state competition in Salt Lake. Anyway, I gotta run, see you at lunch." She hung up.

Bud was so surprised that he didn't even feel the water seeping into the tops of his boots. Pierre and Hoppie had bailed and climbed out of the ditch, not wanting to go swimming, and were standing watching Bud, who finally came to his senses and also climbed out.

He stood there for a bit, feeling happy, then took the clicker from his pocket. He'd been carrying it for almost a week and hadn't even tried it out on the dogs yet.

"Pierre, come," he commanded, clicking the clicker. Pierre ignored Bud, watching a butterfly instead.

"OK, Pierre, stay," Bud said, clicking again. This time, Pierre did as he said.

"Hoppie, your turn. Good boy, Hoppie, stay."

Hoppie was all excited to hear Bud and came running to him, jumping up and getting Bud's khaki pants all muddy.

"Good boy, little Hoppiekins. That's really what I meant, come. You read my mind."

Bud grinned, leading the dogs to the FJ. He'd go home a bit early and kick back before Wilma Jean came home for lunch. It would be nice for a change, after these past few days with Howie.

Just then, Bud's phone rang, and the caller ID said it was Howie. He really didn't want to answer, but he felt guilty, so he decided to keep it short.

"Yell-ow."

"Sheriff, you out irrigating?"

Bud was instantly suspicious. He knew Howie was about to ask him something, and he figured it would end up meaning more escapades. Bud was tired of escapades, and besides, Howie really didn't need his help now that the shenanigans with Gary and Wanda were over.

"I am, Howie. What's up?"

"Oh, I just wondered if you'd mind going with me up to Price. I want to go back and pay Mrs. Mills another visit."

Bud groaned. He'd forgotten all about George being poisoned. Of course, Howie had to follow up on that, but Bud wasn't so sure he needed to go along. But he then thought of the photography exhibit. It would be nice to go see his photo hanging there. Maybe he'd take a picture of it.

Bud replied, "OK, but I can't go until after lunch, Howie. I promised Wilma Jean I'd come home."

"What time should I come by?"

"How's about around 1:30? That'll give me lots of time to recover from the big rabbit lunch we're going to have."

"You're having rabbit for lunch?" Howie asked. "I thought you guys were vegetarians now."

"No, we're having rabbit food. Say, let's stop at the No Delay later, or maybe even the Cowboy Kitchen."

"Maureen gave up on me. We're back to normal now. Oh, and Sheriff, those black market guys are in the Radium County jail, since the quarry's technically in Radium County. I talked to your friend down there, Sheriff Hum Stocks, and he said he would be working out a plea bargain with the D.A. for Gary. You might want to give him a call and see what that's gonna be, cause I'm sure worried about his dogs."

"I'll do that," said Bud. "I feel the same way."

Bud threw his shovel into the back of the farm pickup, then loaded up the dogs and headed for the bungalow, anxious to see what Wilma Jean's surprises were, though he wasn't really sure he wanted to know.

Her surprises hadn't been all that great lately, with the exception of the news about the photo contest, of course. Just yesterday she'd brought a book for him to read from the library called, "Take Control of Your Own Happiness by Being Your Own Child," and it said you should treat yourself with the same kindness you would a child, so maybe he'd do just that, take control of his own surprises and surprise himself with a new video camera.

Bud put the pickup into gear and backed around, almost putting it into the ditch, but not even noticing. He couldn't wait to get home to check out video cameras on the internet. It would be his reward for winning the Grand Prize. Maybe he had some photography talent after all, he thought, and who knows where it might take him.

CHAPTER 39

Bud was sitting in his big easy chair, feeling a bit over-whelmed by all the video camera choices on the internet, when he heard Wilma Jean drive up.

He hoped she had something good for lunch with her, as he was getting hungry. An earlier look in the fridge had revealed only that things were getting desperate on the food front, as all that was in there was a couple of plastic bottles of some kind of grass smoothie—wheatgrass, it was called.

It was bad enough eating like a rabbit, Bud thought, but he sure as heck wasn't going to start eating like a cow, so he'd passed on that and made himself a cup of coffee instead, though it didn't taste the same without the vanilla bean ice cream.

He could see his wife was carrying something, so he jumped up and ran to open the kitchen door for her. The dogs greeted her with wagging tails, and Bud noticed for the umpteenth time that little Pierre never grabbed onto Wilma Jean's pant leg like he did Bud's, dragging along and growling. It made Bud feel a bit persecuted when he had first noticed this, but Wilma Jean had told him it was a kind of special treatment reserved just for him, which made him feel a little better.

Wilma Jean had made a quick run to the grocery store, and Bud couldn't believe his eyes when she put a gallon of vanilla bean ice cream into the freezer.

"You can go to the store tomorrow and do a real run," she told him. "These are just a few things to tide you over."

Bud noted she'd also bought a package of baloney and some cheese.

Now Wilma Jean opened a plastic sack that had the words "Melon Rind Takeout" printed on it.

"I brought you lunch from the cafe," she said, handing him a styrofoam take-out container with a lid. "Just so you know, as soon as these styrofoam plates run out, I'm ordering eco-friendly ones. We're also going to start offering more vegetarian and even vegan dishes. You can come down there when you get tired of eating like a typical American."

Bud wondered if Ray down at the No Delay had ratted on him for eating things like Plucked Dumplings. Someone must have, and Wilma Jean seemed a bit miffed about it.

He was half-afraid to open the take-out plate, but he popped up the lid. He couldn't believe his eyes—it was a hot roast-beef sandwich with creamy mashed potatoes and a small salad on the side!

Wilma Jean patted him on the head as she handed him some silverware, saying, "This is one of the surprises I mentioned. I'm worried about your diet—you're the only person I know who can put on weight while eating vegetarian, so I think you should go back to eating like normal. But Hon, please try a little harder to eat more fruit and veggies, OK?"

Bud nodded his head in agreement, trying to smile, but his mouth was too full.

Wilma Jean continued. "And now for the other surprise I mentioned. Your buddy Larry up in Elmo has been trying to get ahold of you, and apparently he had the wrong number or something, but he finally called down at the cafe. He's getting married this weekend and wants you to be his best man. Some artist gal named Alberta from Marin, and she sounds like the total opposite of him, so it should work out well. Howie and his band are playing the reception, and your old friends Doc Richardson and Millie from the Ghost Rock Cafe will be there. But you'll need to get up to Price immediately and rent a tux."

Bud almost choked on his food at this news. Larry getting married? It was the last thing he would have predicted. And for the crusty truck driver to marry a California gal—wasn't everyone from northern California pretty much a bleeding-heart liberal? As far as Bud remembered, Larry was a member of the NRA and voted Independent, when he voted at all.

It then struck him that Wilma Jean had said something about renting a tuxedo. Bud had never worn a tux in his life, in fact, he wasn't sure he'd ever even seen anyone else wearing one, except in pictures in things like People Magazine and such, which he read only when in the dentist's waiting room.

This news started to make him lose his appetite, but he quickly recovered. Howie would soon be there to pick him up, so he started a pot of coffee, then sat back down to finish his lunch, saving a few bites for Hoppie and Pierre.

Wilma Jean left just as Howie drove up. Bud put a few dollops of ice cream in the thermos, filled it with coffee, and headed out the door. For once, he was looking forward to going up to Price, as he couldn't wait to see his photo with the big purple ribbon on it.

Then he remembered the tux. Oh well, he would just have to get used to the idea, after all, Larry would do the same for him—maybe, anyway, though he sure couldn't picture Larry in a tux.

Bud was now feeling even more hesitant than before. He sure couldn't picture himself wearing such a contraption, and he wondered why it was even necessary. Wasn't his old tweed jacket good enough? It just didn't seem like something Larry would require, but it was probably the doing of Larry's future wife, since women were usually in charge of planning weddings. If men were, they'd all just get married in whatever they happened to be wearing, if they got married at all.

Bud got into Howie's Land Cruiser and they drove off, just like they had every day for pretty much a week now.

"Sheriff, I need a raise," Bud joked.

Howie looked panicked for a moment, then answered, "Bud, I'll have to talk to the mayor. Or maybe you should talk to the mayor, since you know him better. After all, you were sheriff for five years, and I just started. You'd have better luck asking than I would, I think."

"Tell you what," Bud said. "Let's just consider it a contribution to my public duty, as long as you buy the gas. I need to go to Price anyway. You suppose the sheriff's office would mind running me around a bit on some personal business once we get there?"

"Not at all," Howie said, still looking serious. "Don't even think twice about it. It's the least I can do."

"OK, our first stop will be the museum."

"The museum? You mean the one with the big metal Utahraptor out front?" Howie asked.

"Yup. I have a little surprise for you."

"I hope it isn't something that will do me in like that Utahraptor would if it could," Howie grinned.

"I don't know about that, Howie, but I don't think you need to worry too much," Bud replied.

CHAPTER 40

Bud and Howie pulled into the museum parking lot, then got out and stood under the big life-size metal Utahraptor which had some poor unfortunate smaller metal dinosaur in its big metal teeth.

This was the one thing Bud didn't like about dinosaurs, it seemed like they were always eating each other, and he didn't like to watch dinosaur movies for the same reason. Seemed like they all just lived to eat. It made him hungry, and he'd just eaten only an hour before.

They both put a few bucks into the donation box, then followed the signs that led to the photography display in a back room. Bud started to get a knot in his stomach.

It took awhile to find his photo, and Howie didn't help things much by having to examine every photo on the way, but Bud finally saw his photo of the big Amtrak engine fading into the sunset with the Bookcliffs glowing red in the distance.

Sure enough, it had a big Grand Champion ribbon hanging off it, and Bud was now about ready to tear up. He hoped Howie wouldn't notice.

"Wow, Sheriff, is that your photo? You mean you're the Grand Champion of the whole show? Wow." Howie seemed really impressed.

Bud was speechless and just stood there for a long time. He then finally started wandering around, looking at the other entries. He liked a colorful one of quilts and thought it maybe was better than his, but he sure wasn't going to argue with the judges. He then found a sign that listed who the judges were, and there, right before his eyes, was the name Judge Richter.

This took the wind from his sails a bit, as he knew Judge Richter was a real judge, the kind who hangs out in courtrooms, and he was the same one who'd befriended his Uncle Junior when he'd been on his recent hobo jaunt, riding the rails. That particular judge was also an avid railroad buff. Bud now knew why he'd won the competition, and he felt a bit deflated.

Bud and Howie now walked into the Hall of Vertebrates, where a giant mastodon was center stage. The skeleton had been uncovered when excavating a reservoir up above Huntington, not too far from Price, and it was definitely the main star of the museum.

Howie was now standing in front of a glass display, and he motioned for Bud to come over. There appeared to be a sort of garden behind the glass with a sign that read "Poisonous Plants of Our Region."

Bud and Howie both stood there for a bit, and Bud recognized a few of the plants, like locoweed, or Astragalus. Each plant had a little placard that told a bit about it.

He looked at a beautiful purple-blue plant that reminded him a little of the penstemon that Wilma Jean had tried to plant last year in the garden but that hadn't survived Hoppie's digging.

The placard read, "Aconitum, also known as the queen of poisons, is also called aconite, monkshood, wolf's bane,

leopard's bane, devil's helmet, or blue rocket, and is a
genus of over 250 species of flowering plants belonging to
the family Ranunculaceae. These herbaceous perennials
are natives of the mountainous parts of the northern hemi-
sphere, growing in mountain meadows."

Bud just stood there for a bit as what he'd just read
started to sink in.

"Look, Howie, isn't this the same plant George had just
transplanted into his garden from Bruin Point?"

Howie read the placard and stood there silent for
awhile. Finally, he said, "George poisoned himself accidentally from handling the plant. It wasn't murder at all."

Bud nodded grimly. "I guess we should go by there and
tell his wife and dig the stuff up—with gloves."

They continued to walk around a bit, the fact that
George had accidentally poisoned himself still sinking in,
neither paying much attention to the museum displays.

Bud now knew what his dream had been trying to tell
him—he'd somehow made the connection in his subconscious between the monkshood in George's garden and the
man's death, and thus his dream where the flowers killed
the alien that looked like George.

He and Howie had pretty much decided they should
go when Bud noticed someone out of the corner of his eye
over behind a saber-toothed tiger skeleton, someone he
thought he knew.

He grabbed Howie and pulled him behind a big display
of Fremont pots, then whispered, "Cherokee Smith's over
there."

"Oh man, Sheriff," Howie whispered back, "I bet he's in
here trying to figure out what kind of dino skeleton to dig
up next. That guy is totally suspicious."

"Agreed," Bud whispered back. "Let's get out of here."

They tried to sneak out, but it was only seconds later that Cherokee spotted them.

"Hey, it's my old flying buddy, the Sheriff of Emery County, and his sidekick," the man bellowed out. "What are you boys doing up here? Man, am I glad to see you, Sheriff. I felt real bad about what happened to George Mills. He's a buddy of Colt's, and I was giving him an air tour. He wanted me to let him off there and come back later, wanted to go rockhounding, but my plane conked out, as you know. I called his wife after I got back into town, but she said he'd been found by you guys. Anyway, come on back with me, I want to introduce you to my clients."

Cherokee practically dragged Howie into a back hallway that led to several offices, then through the door of one with a sign that said "Staff Only." Bud trailed along, pretty much unnoticed.

There sat the two men who had been following them in the white state pickup and the red Jeep.

Cherokee said to the pair as he pointed to Howie, "This here's the guy who rescued that girl in the Black Box I was telling you about. He's sheriff of Green River."

"We've met before. I'm Colt Bryant," said Colt, standing and shaking Howie's hand. The other man also shook Howie's hand and said, "I'm Jesse Kirk. I've seen you at the No Delay Cafe. Nice to finally meet you. How does it feel to make a major dinosaur discovery?"

Howie looked shocked. "Me? I think you're confusing me with someone else."

"No, Cherokee took us to the dig site you told him about. We hired him to help us find it. We've been looking for it for over a year, ever since we realized someone was selling claws on the black market. Colt bought a few at Tucson and brought them back, and we could tell from some of the matrix still on them that they came from Cedar Mountain Formation and were a new species. We just got back from the dig, and once we excavate it and know more about what we have, the dino will be named after you."

Howie started to stutter. "But I didn't..."

Bud interrupted him. "Howie showed me the site after he found it, and it's obviously had some digging. You have any idea who did that?"

Colt answered, "No, I wish we did. We've been trying to find whoever was selling the claws, even had a BLM agent at the last Tucson Show, but we never did figure it out. They must've been going out there at night and were pretty darn careful about not being seen. Too bad, because if they'd been straight up and reported it when they found it, they'd be listed as the finder and have the dino named after them."

"Well, congratulations, Sheriff," Bud said to Howie, grinning. "Not everyone gets a dino named after them. You guys have any idea what it is exactly?"

Now Jesse answered. "I'm the state archaeologist, have been for years, and I've never seen anything like it. It's a Therizinosaur, but more of a hybrid between a meat-eater and a vegetarian than the others we've found, plus it has unmistakable evidence of feathers. It's the most primitive Therizinosaur yet discovered. It's quite a find. We'll probably name it the Falcarius howiensis."

Bud replied, "So that's why you guys were following us around?"

Colt answered, "Yeah, and you sure didn't make it easy, changing vehicles all the time. What exactly were you doing, anyway?"

Bud laughed. "We were actually on a missing person case. But why would you follow a sheriff's vehicle? Did you think the sheriff would steal bones?"

"We didn't know," Jesse replied. "We have to suspect anything in this kind of deal. When there's big bucks involved, even the law isn't necessarily above the law, if you know what I mean. A new kind of dinosaur would sell for up to a million dollars or more to the right collector."

Howie stood silent, as if in shock. Finally, he said to Bud, "Well, I said I hoped the surprise wouldn't do me in, but it sure is." He paused, trying to control his feelings, then asked, "Anyway, which one of you lost the meteorite? I have it out in my truck."

Colt was surprised. "No way! You found it? You just earned a thousand-dollar reward, Sheriff."

Howie again started stuttering. "No, no need to pay me..."

Colt said, "Sheriff, that reward is yours and you deserve it. That's a very rare meteorite, and if it had fallen into the wrong hands..."

Now Jesse added, "The museum had just purchased it. It's a so-called carbonaceous chondrite. It contains dust granules that may have been part of the cloud of material that came together to form our Solar System. It's a very important piece of research material. Colt was worried sick about it, so please take the reward. You deserve it."

Colt was excited. "Where is it?" He then turned to Bud and said, "Oh, by the way, I reported that can dump you discovered to the BLM. They say it's quite a find, lots of old historic junk in it. They know who you are and are calling it the Shumway Dump. Thought you might like to know."

Bud walked out the door after Howie and Colt, trying to ignore the grin on Cherokee's face.

CHAPTER 41

Bud and Howie sat in the back booth of the No Delay Cafe, eating apple pie a la mode. Bud was already seeing a slight weight loss, now that he didn't have to always worry about starving to death, which had made him want to eat more than he needed. This made Wilma Jean happy, and all was well on the home front.

Except for the tuxedo, that is, the one he and Howie had just driven up to Price to return. Bud had been the only one at Larry's wedding wearing a tux, and this had made him the star of the party, much to his despair. He had taken a lot of ribbing, and Larry seemed to think it was hilarious.

So much for Wilma Jean's assumptions, and Bud knew it wouldn't be the last time he would be the victim of such. He supposed it was part of his wedding vows, though Wilma Jean seemed to have gotten the best of the deal, as Bud never assumed much of anything. Well, maybe that was wrong, he thought, as he liked to suppose she would cook for him once in awhile—and real food, not this vegetarian stuff. That reminded him that she had promised meatballs for dinner, so he'd better leave some room.

Wanda now came from the kitchen and sat down by Howie. Gary followed, wearing the "She Who Must Be Obeyed" apron.

"How's it going, Gary?" Bud asked.

Gary smiled. "I did a plea bargain and only got six months' probation. But no more digging, cause part of the deal is if I dig anymore, I go to jail. But I'm gonna start working in the Bone Lab up at the museum—that'll get it out of my system, and I'll get to work with real paleontologists. That was part of the plea bargain, a year working there 10 hours a week, no pay. That seems more like fun than a sentence, if you ask me. Your sheriff friend down there is sure a nice guy, Bud."

"That's great, Gary, glad to hear it. But where's Ray?" Bud asked.

Wanda answered, "He's on vacation, over at the trailer. He says my absence wore him out, so me and Gary are taking over for a few days, plus, he has to go supervise the new projects."

"What new projects?" Howie asked.

"We're getting a new sign," Wanda replied. "It's way bigger and flashes, and that should draw people in like flies. The trucker who hit the old one, his insurance is paying for it. Plus—and you won't believe this—the highway department has finally decided to put in a turn lane. They said they'd be out tomorrow to start the work."

"What made them decide to do that?" Bud asked.

"I dunno," Wanda said. "But I think it's because one of their head honchos stopped in and almost got hit. At least that's the rumor I heard. It was while I was out missing."

Gary snorted. "You weren't out missing, you were right here the whole time and everyone knows it."

Wanda looked annoyed. "I wasn't here *all* the time. I still rode Buck out every day, and I sure spent way too much time up at your junky place, trying to keep from getting killed by the company you keep."

She reflected for a minute, then said, "Speaking of company, you know that theater company up in Price, the Pearls of Great Price? I auditioned and got accepted for their next drama. I'm going to play the part of an old scruffy miner this time, but the director told me I'd make a great Baby Doe Tabor, and that's the next play."

"Who's that?" Gary asked.

"Baby Doe? She was the beautiful wife of one of the old-time silver barons over in Colorado and a very colorful person. You'll just have to come to the play, Gary, and get some culture. Wouldn't hurt you a bit, though I know you think it would."

"Well, you sure had us all fooled, Wanda," Howie said. "I think you're a great actor. I just hope you give up on those cigars."

Wanda laughed. "That was just part of the act. Ray's really proud of me, at least after he got over being mad. But when I explained that my life was in danger, he was OK. And when I told him about my idea to have Howie and the Ramblin' Road Rangers come play square dances every Saturday night, he was totally happy. He sure doesn't take me for granted anymore. This place is really gonna come around, and with Gary now helping out, bring it on. But we need to get back to work. You boys have a nice day, and thanks for all your help."

Wanda disappeared into the kitchen with Gary trailing behind.

Bud looked at Howie. "You're going to play square dances?"

Howie beamed. "Yeah, and I'm gonna be sure to mention it when the newspaper comes out to interview me. Try to get some free publicity."

"The newspaper?" Bud asked.

"Well," Howie replied, "Actually maybe several newspapers and even a TV station."

Bud whistled. "Wow, that sounds impressive. They're coming to our little town of Green River?"

"Yup," Howie said, beaming. "Tomorrow. They want to cover the rescue of Lillian—I'm getting a commendation from the Utah Sheriff's Association. Plus they want to cover the arrest of the bone diggers and the new dinosaur named after me."

He hesitated, then said, "You know, Bud, I really think they should name it after you."

Bud replied, "No, no, you know me, I don't like being in the limelight. That should go to someone who would enjoy it more, and Howie, you were right there beside me when we found it, anyway."

"That's awfully nice of you, Sheriff," Howie said. "Think about it—Wilma Jean just told me I won her naming contest with my Tumbleweed Alley, and I got that big reward for finding the meteorite. And I just got a nice box of chocolate toffee from George Mill's wife. I guess I'm doing OK, huh, Sheriff?"

"I'm impressed," Bud replied. "Have you told Maureen about all this?"

Howie said, "Not yet. I'm gonna wait and show her the newspaper article, have her watch the TV news. But Bud..." He paused.

"Go on, Howie."

"Well, that's just not bad for someone with a ten-cent brain, is it?"

Bud laughed, and they got up and paid the bill.

"It's not bad at all, Howie, not bad at all," Bud replied, clicking the clicker in his pocket.

They both walked out the door and on to better things.

• • •

About the Author

Chinle Miller writes from southeastern Utah, where she spends most of her time wandering with her dogs, eyeing civilization from a safe distance. She has a B.A. in Anthropology and an M.A. in Linguistics and is currently working on a degree in geology.

If you enjoyed this book, you'll also enjoy the first book in the Bud Shumway mystery series, *The Ghost Rock Cafe*, as well as the second, *The Slickrock Cafe,* and the third, *The Paradox Cafe*. And don't miss *Desert Rats: Adventures in the American Outback* and *Uranium Daughter*, both by Chinle Miller.

And if you enjoy Bigfoot stories, you'll love *Rusty Wilson's Bigfoot Campfire Stories* and his many other Bigfoot books, available in paperback or as ebooks from yellowcatbooks.com and your favorite online retailer.

You can also find unique Bigfoot hats and apparel at yellowcatbooks.com.

• • •

Made in the USA
San Bernardino, CA
19 July 2017